FOR THE LOVE OF FRITTERS & FRIGHTS

J.D. LINTON

To those who just need a good laugh and a good fuck on Halloween.

PREFACE

CONTENT WARNING:

For the Love of Fritters & Frights is a fun, romantic Halloween novella, but it does contain some elements that may not be suitable for some readers including explicit sexual content, profanity, and blood.

Readers who may be sensitive to these elements, please take note.

HALLOW FALL'S CALENDER

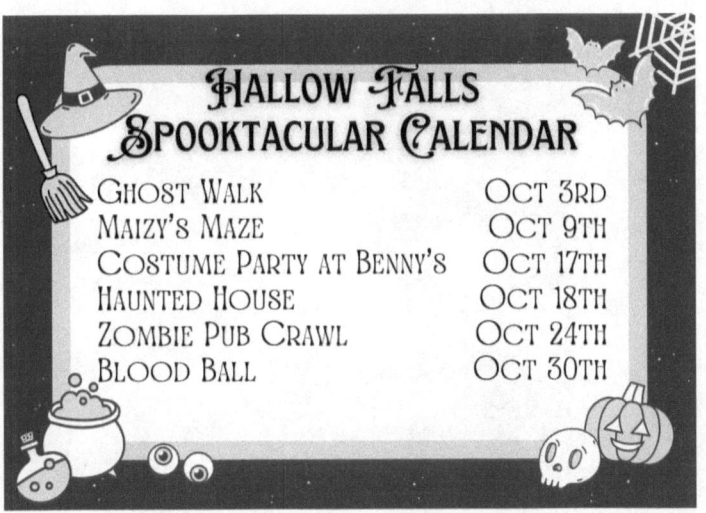

Hallow Falls Spooktacular Calendar

Ghost Walk	Oct 3rd
Maizy's Maze	Oct 9th
Costume Party at Benny's	Oct 17th
Haunted House	Oct 18th
Zombie Pub Crawl	Oct 24th
Blood Ball	Oct 30th

I

DON'T CRY OVER SPILLED COFFEE

Leaves crunched underfoot, creating a scatter of orange and red over the worn sidewalk. A stiff breeze swirled them into the crisp air; the scent of firewood and changing weather floated along with them.

A colorful array of mums and pumpkins decorated the sidewalk to Books and Boos. Aggie, an old witch, owned the bookshop, and let her oldest and dearest friend sell her mead there—hence, the booze.

Honestly, there's no better combination. I smiled as I rounded the corner to Main Street. Her shop was in the corner building—a small, ancient bookstore that smelled of candles, apples, and old paper. It was my happy place, and I volunteered there every Saturday. Aggie didn't need the help, but she accepted me with open arms every time.

I waited at the crosswalk until the light turned then darted across, narrowly missing a taxi that ran the light.

"My apologies, Remi," the taxi driver shouted from his window.

"No biggie," I called back with a shrug, waving as he passed by.

Hard to tell the color of the light when they didn't have eyes. He was one of the headless horsemen—or used to be. They didn't ride horses anymore, but they were still headless.

The door to Books and Boos was already propped open with Pum sitting on the wooden bench next to it, curled up on the orange blanket that was thrown over the corner. Pumpkin, or Pum for short, was Aggie's orange tabby cat and her soul tie. He went everywhere she did, but he loved the bookstore and the patrons' accompanying pets the most.

I sat on the bench beside him, and he crawled into my lap, running his head along my hand as Aggie and Maggie stepped out. They were both dressed in long, flowing dresses, topped with velvet shawls.

"October first," Aggie hummed with a contented sigh. She handed me a mug of steaming apple cider and plopped down beside me.

"The first day of the best month." Maggie, her best friend, sat on the arm of the bench. "I have a feeling *this* October may be a little sweeter than most."

I raised a brow and blew on the steaming liquid. Her 'feelings' were never wrong. "What makes you say that?"

She smiled at me. "I guess we'll have to wait and see."

I laughed and sipped the cider, sighing as the warmth slid down my throat, and Pum purred, curling up on my lap. I tipped my head back, closing my eyes and inhaling deeply as the crisp breeze blew again.

"It feels amazing out today," I said.

"Aye, it does," Aggie replied. "An echo of the weather to come."

"So, what jobs do you have for me today?"

"We have a box of books to be put out if you're up for it. Old ones, they are. Grimoires and the like."

"Oh, sure. My hands are yours for the day," I joked, holding them up to her.

"Careful what you say, deary. Say that to a witch with ill intentions, and you may find yourself without hands for a day," Maggie said, and Aggie threw her head back in laughter.

"Shall I take them, then?" Aggie teased, nudging her friend.

I swatted her arm. "As long as I get them back."

"That seems fair enough...But I'll let you keep them. This time." She winked and sighed, dropping her eyes to her mug with a soft smile. "My grandson is coming for a visit. He should be arriving today. I haven't seen him in ages. Not since he was but a wee teenager."

"Oh, that's nice," I replied. "How long is he going to be in town?"

"Well, he's never had the pleasure of a full October in Hallow Falls, so I managed to talk him into staying for the whole month." Her smile widened, deepening the wrinkles around her eyes and revealing her endearingly crooked teeth. "Would you mind if he stayed at the Dead and Breakfast? I would pay ya, of course."

"Oh, of course, he can stay. I have plenty of rooms available, and I don't usually start booking up until closer to Halloween, anyway. And please, no money. Your company, free books, and"—I raised the mug—"cider is plenty."

"For a month's stay? I'll be owing you cider for the rest of our very long lives."

"Good, because I don't plan on going anywhere. You're stuck with me, you old hag."

She laughed, and Pum lifted his head to her. "Well, I'll be here. Every Saturday. With cider and work ready for ya."

"Sounds perfect to me."

THE AIR HAD WARMED a bit by lunch but not enough to chase the slight chill as I strolled to the coffee shop down the street to finish off my time in town before heading back to the Dead and Breakfast.

The sidewalks were bustling, every face smiling and excited for the month. Hallow Falls thrived in October, which wasn't a surprise considering we were a town of what we called misfits, but the humans called monsters. They wrote their stories and legends about our misunderstood ancestors from centuries ago, but the citizens of our small town were tucked away, safe and hidden from the humans, long since chalked up to fairy tales.

The only humans who came here were those with the intention to find us. If they didn't know of our existence, our small town was nothing but a forest on either side of a long, desolate highway. A small blip on the map.

But for those who came looking—with *good* intentions, of course—we were here to be found, happy and welcoming to all.

As I neared the coffee shop, I stopped, swallowing hard as my eyes dropped to study my outfit, internally groaning. It was wash day, and I was wearing my worst jeans and a ratty T-shirt. Not to mention I don't even think I brushed my hair before I threw it up in a bun.

Eddy, the owner of the local dog shelter and unknowing

love of my life, was walking this way with a few of his dogs. He was a 6'5" grizzly of a man. With long, shaggy brown hair, a beard that he couldn't keep shaved, and a red flannel buttoned but revealing his muscled chest as it was tightly molded to his form, he was carved by the gods—a very perfect representation of what a werewolf was supposed to be.

He was delicious...and I was wearing my rattiest clothes.

Someone opened the door and I ducked inside with my eyes glued to Eddy as he knelt down to pet the overgrown German shepherd. I sighed, my head tilting to the side, and bumped straight into someone with at least two hot coffees, judging by the burning liquid that ran down both our fronts.

I hissed and jumped back as it soaked through my shirt —my white shirt. Gasping, I slid a hand over my chest as I crouched down to grab one of the cups.

"I'm so sorry about that. You'd think a vampire would have more awareness about her," I mumbled to the person whose day I just ruined.

"No worries," he said, and I glanced up.

He was new in town, and we didn't see many new faces. Not unless it was Halloween night—and it was a bit too early for that.

I stood, tossing the empty cup in the trash bin. "Please let me buy you some new coffee. You probably didn't even get a chance to taste it yet."

"I tasted it...once," he said, laughing.

I grinned. "That settles it. Come on." I walked past him to the ordering counter.

"One dirty chai latte and...?" I turned to my stranger.

"Just one black coffee," he chimed in. He was much

taller than me—which wasn't saying much considering I was five foot nothing—but as he leaned over my shoulder, I had to crane my neck to look up at him.

"You definitely had two coffees based on how much I spilled on the both of us," I whispered up at him.

He grinned down at me. "All right. Two black coffees," he said to the cashier.

I paid and walked to the waiting corner with him as my shadow.

"I'm Remi, by the way." I started to pull my right hand away from my shirt to shake his but stopped, my cheeks flushing furiously. Sliding my left hand over my breasts—now on full display thanks to my soaked shirt—I extended a hand.

He slid his into mine. "Jack."

"Well, nice to meet you, Jack. You're new in town, right?"

"What gave me away?"

"We don't get many new faces, so those we do...tend to stick out."

He nodded, stifling a smile that revealed a deep dimple in his tan cheek. Black hair hung over his forehead just above brilliant blue eyes.

"Yeah, I'm new...ish. I've been here before a few times, but what better place to spend October than Hallow Falls?" He waved a hand to the barista as she set our drinks on the bar.

"I couldn't agree more." He handed me my chai. "Thanks," I said as I popped the lid off and blew on it.

"Be careful." The seriousness in his tone caught my attention, and my brows furrowed as I peeked up at him. "Without a lid on. I wouldn't want ya to spill that one, too."

I scrunched my nose. "Oh, for the love of fritters and

frights. Take your coffee and be gone. Go," I teased, waving him out the door. "Go explore. Go shop. Go anywhere but here, so I can live in peace without the reminder."

His form shook with laughter as he strolled out the door, glancing at me through the shop glass. He lifted the cup in farewell and walked out of sight.

2

FRIENDS THAT GO BUMP IN THE NIGHT

The bell above the coffee shop door chimed again, pulling my attention from my book just as Eddy filled the doorway.

I could've sworn my still heart nearly thumped at the sight. My hands frantically smoothed my hair as I glanced down to check myself and bit back a groan at the drying brown stain, feeling the burn seep into my cheeks.

He threw one hand in the air and waved while tugging his pups inside with the other. "Hey, Remi."

"Hi, Ed." I stood and stepped toward him, but of course, my foot hooked on the leg of a chair and sent me tumbling forward.

I caught myself on a table to my side, and the blush in my cheeks deepened to an embarrassing red. With a huff, I stood *again,* pushing the loose hair away from my face. Eddy was frozen, his mouth hanging slack before twisting into a grin, and he covered it with his hand.

"Can we pretend you didn't see that?" I whispered as I passed by him on my way to the door.

"See what?" he asked behind me.

"Exactly."

The glass door slowly closed behind me, and I strolled down the sidewalk with feigned confidence until I was finally out of sight, then dropped my forehead to my palm and sighed.

"Nearly ate shit twice in one day," I mumbled. Why was it that clumsiness only presented itself in times when it could be incredibly embarrassing or annoying—or both? If I was destined to trip my way into eternity, why couldn't it just be in the comfort of my own home where no one else could witness it?

Stopping at the curb of the sidewalk, I checked for any rogue cabs and darted across the street into Shadow Park.

It was beautiful this time of year. The trees were various shades of orange and red; carved pumpkins and large candle-lit lanterns lined the cracked cobblestone path. Cobwebs stretched over the entryway gate with Mr. Ambercup Pumpkinhead's spider babies taking up residence. They were adorable, creeping and crawling over their Halloween homes.

Ambercup stepped into view, carrying a massively overgrown pumpkin. He was spindly, his arms and legs as thin as the branches he cared for. He was the park's caregiver and he did his job wonderfully.

His orange head turned to me, his carved mouth morphing into a grin. "Hello, Remi. Is the Dead and Breakfast participating in the Ghost Walk this year?"

"I still need to talk to Robert and Eliza, but you know they'll want to. They always do."

"Kind spirits they are, and ridiculously lucky to have you as their decorator." His hollow eyes lit with soft, flickering light. "Although, I think the park is going to give you a run for your money. I've been growing these babies all year."

He sat the pumpkin by the others along the path, a terrifying smile carved on its face.

"They look fantastic, Amber."

"Well, thank you, lass, but that's not the best part. Watch this." He winked and leaned forward, running a bony finger over the curve of the pumpkin, and it blinked.

"What? That has to be cheating!" I laughed as he ran down the path, running his finger over the top of each one. They woke one at a time, all grinning and studying their surroundings.

Once he had animated all of his pumpkins, he turned back to me and shrugged his shoulders. "Can't make first place too easy for ya."

"No, you're definitely not. This is too cool."

He looped an awkwardly long arm through mine as we walked down the worn path. "Speaking of cool, how's Eddy?"

"Oh, he's cool. Fine. Handsome... Delicious. Same old, same old. Although, I highly doubt he thinks the same of me. I nearly busted my ass this morning."

"Again?"

I groaned and ran a hand down my face.

"You'd think a vampire would be better on her feet."

"You'd think so," I sighed, flushing as I relived the mortification. "So, when is the Ghost Walk this year, the second or the third?"

"Sundown, not tomorrow but the next day."

"So the third." I chuckled and nodded. "All right. That'll give me plenty of time to top this."

He laughed—a deep, rumbling sound. "Yeah, right. I can't wait to see what you come up with."

The Ghost Walk was our annual fundraiser for those transitioning from living to dead to undead. It was an amazing program, matching newly transitioned ghosts to their forever haunts. It was how Robert and Eliza found me and the Dead and Breakfast, so the organization had a special place in our hearts. They had become two of my closest friends over the past few decades as well as my permanent residents, and that was exactly why we went all out every year—Eliza especially, winning us first place for over ten years running.

I couldn't help but smile to myself. She'd always been competitive, even in the afterlife, but hey, at least it was all in good *spirits*.

Stifling a laugh, I asked, "I haven't decided what baked goods to donate to the sale this year, though. Any suggestions?"

"Pumpkin fritters." He moaned dramatically. "Or Hell's bells, pumpkin bread. Yes, bread."

I peeked up at him. "Isn't that...I don't know...cannibalism?"

He laughed again. "I was born, thank you. Not grown from the ground as they are. We're not related. It's just an uncanny resemblance."

"Yeah, born of the vine," I teased.

He nudged me with his elbow. "I'm going to tell my mother you said that."

"Oh, you know I'm just kidding."

"Sure, but I'll still accept a loaf of pumpkin bread as an apology."

"I'll bring you two for good measure."

"You're too good to me," he groaned, rubbing a hand over his stomach as we reached the other end of the park.

The Dead and Breakfast sat across the street, as beautiful and dark and haunted as I'd left it.

"And don't you forget it." I winked, pointing a finger at him as I walked backward through the gate before turning and jogging across the empty street.

As I stepped over the threshold, I stopped to take a deep breath. With the sun sinking on the horizon, the air was chilled and clear—my preferred weather. The moon was bright and full overhead, its band of stars twinkling in admiration of our sweet little town.

A shooting star shot across the sky then, so I closed my eyes and made my wish. Humans might make wishes among them, but it wouldn't work unless they truly believed in them. Those stars were vain, fickle little things, and they only granted wishes to those who feed into their ego. They needed faith in their ability, and a compliment or two never hurt.

"You're the brightest star I've ever seen," I whispered to the sky.

It glowed brighter and faded from sight. *Well, at least it heard me.*

I examined the house as I strolled up the front walk to the porch. With just pumpkins and mums placed on the steps, it would need a good bit of work to earn another Ghost Walk win.

Fred walked around the corner with his toolbox, moving at his normally slow pace. He was tall—seven feet easily—and as green as the ground he came from. Fred was a part of the undead community, although he wasn't a ghost or a vampire like me. He was a zombie.

Contrary to popular belief, they didn't actually chase and feast on humans. They were *much* too slow for that. A small child could walk faster than he could run. They preferred the already dead and decaying, typically opting for animals they found throughout the forests, or even on the side of the road. Zombies did a pretty damn good job at keeping the streets of Hallow Falls clean.

"Hello, Fred," I said, stepping back down the stairs.

"Well, hi there, Remi," he replied at a pace that matched his achingly slow steps.

"Something need maintenance today?"

"Ah." He lifted his toolbox. "Just a leaky pipe. All better now, though."

"Thanks." I hooked a thumb towards the front door. "I'm going to speak with Robert and Eliza about the Ghost Walk. Want to join?"

He nodded, climbing the steps one at a time. "Of course."

As we entered, we found Robert and Eliza sipping tea in the foyer.

"Well, I'll be! It's about time you made it home." Eliza shot to her feet, her hazy form nearly opaque. "We're really cutting it close this year. We need to pick a theme for the house."

"El is quite excited for the Walk this year," Robert said, rising to join her.

"Aren't I always?" She cracked a grin at him.

He threw an arm around her shoulders, and she beamed as he pulled her into his side. They were as in love now as much as they were in life—not a rare occurrence among ghosts but still heartwarming all the same.

"Well, what did you have in mind?"

"I know we usually pick a specific theme, but we were thinking for this year, let's just do Halloween—like cozy, early 2000's, bright and colorful Halloween. We can have bowls of candy and a pumpkin carving area for the kids, smoke machines, a little radio playing Halloween music. Not scary but wholesome."

My mouth fell slack before curling up in a smile. "That sounds amazing, and I would even bet we still have some old decorations in the attic."

"Perfect," Eliza squealed, clapping her hands.

"Want to pull an all-nighter with me?" I cocked a brow at Eliza. "We can get it all up and ready to go."

"Is that even a question? I'm down like a frown," she said, looping my arm through mine. "Let's go."

3

IT'S RAINING BATS

The attic was as vast as the rest of the house, but dusty and disorganized.

Boxes of everything we could imagine had accumulated over the decades, and it took us a solid hour to find the old Halloween decor, but we had everything we needed. There were dozens of boxes full of lights, pumpkins, skeletons, spiders, everything—more than we could ever use on this house.

"Have you ever gotten rid of anything?" Eliza pulled out a moth-chewed costume from Ghouls knew when. "You're a bit of a pack rat."

"Lucky for you," I said as I lifted an old jack-o-lantern.

She beamed as I handed it to her to toss in the designated basket. "Lucky for *us*."

I opened another tub to find tangled purple and orange lights, twined together with disintegrating fake cobwebs. Suppressing a cringe at how long *that* would take to unwind, I shut the lid and turned to the next box—a smaller one, full of paper bats and spiders.

With a huff, I stood and dusted myself off before

stacking the box atop the lights and picking them both up. As I headed for the attic hatch, I looked back to say, "Be back in a second."

She nodded as she pulled out a small gauzy ghost suspended from a fishing line loop, and a laugh burst from me. She rolled her eyes, pointing to the two black dots on the fabric as it swung from the nail she placed it on, but the smile slid from her face when she glanced up at me.

She jerked forward, but it was too late. "Wait—"

My next step connected with nothing but air. I tumbled forward through the opening with a scream and scrunched my eyes, anticipating the worst, but I landed in strong arms instead, breathing heavily as one of the boxes landed with a thud beside us.

My brows furrowed as I looked into bright blue eyes. Confusion muddled my thoughts along with the scent of spicy cologne seconds before hundreds of tiny, black bats fluttered down around us.

Jack's chest vibrated with a chuckle.

"We have got to stop meeting like this," I mumbled.

His gaze shifted back to me, and I squirmed beneath it.

"Like what?" he asked.

"In the most unconventional and *embarrassing* ways."

Someone cleared their throat behind him, and I jumped before wiggling from his grasp. He sat me on my feet, and we turned to see Aggie who stood mere feet away with a curious smile and her gaze flitting between the two of us.

My Ghouls-forsaken cheeks burned, and she noticed immediately, raising her brows and tilting her head to the side. "Remi, this is my grandson, Jack. Although, it seems you two have already met."

I swiveled toward him, my jaw slack. "You—"

"The Dead and Breakfast is yours?" he asked at the same moment with a lopsided grin.

"Yep." I nodded awkwardly and placed my hands on my hips.

"It's a great little place for a vacation, quiet and warm," Aggie said, "and Remi makes the best baked goods around. You'll be fattened and plumped before you leave in a month's time."

She pinched his muscular arm, and he swatted her hand away.

"Thanks, Aggie," I said with a chuckle, turning back to Jack. "Well, I guess I'll show you to your room, and then come back to clean this up."

Aggie started scooping up paper bats before we'd even made it out of sight, her laughter following us down the hall. It wasn't long before Eliza's laughter joined hers, and I sighed *deeply*, the flush in my cheeks hot as hell fire—an incredibly inconvenient effect that I personally felt should be left to the living. Without a beating heart, I wasn't even sure what possessed the blood within my body to do such a thing. Whatever it was, it was annoying.

It felt like an eternity before we finally made it to Jack's room at the end of the hall. Coming to a stop, I turned and gestured to the open door. "Here you are."

He walked past me into the room, glancing around as he set his suitcase on the bed. "This is...nicer than I expected."

Unsure whether I should be offended or not, I opened my mouth to speak, but he spun on his heel and held a hand up. "In a good way, I promise. A really good way."

I cracked a smile, releasing a breathy laugh. "I'm glad you like it."

With dark walls, antique furniture, and brass candelabras lit with flickering candles, it had always been one of my favorites—usually a guest favorite too.

As he pulled the curtains open, sunlight beamed around him, leaving his form a dark silhouette. I knew that window revealed a beautiful view of Hallow Falls' park, yet all I could see was him. He was massive.

Ghouls, how tall is this guy?

Averting my gaze, I backed out of the room. "Well, breakfast is from six to nine in the morning, but the neighbors usually stop by too, so if you want the good stuff, better come early."

I started down the hall when he stuck his head through the doorway. "Thank you, Remi."

I smiled and peeked over my shoulder. "You're welcome, Jack."

Aggie and Eliza were finishing up with the last few bats when I returned. "You two didn't have to do that. That was my fault."

"Oh, nonsense." Aggie waved a hand through the air. "These haggard bones need a little exercise."

Eliza's form shook with silent laughter as she sat on the steps of the attic ladder.

"I didn't realize he was your grandson. I met him earlier at the coffee shop and..." I glanced up at her, and her eyes were already on me—her *bright blue* eyes. Even her hair was as dark as his, just speckled with gray and white, her skin tanned in the same way his was. I should've made the connection. "Well, I'm guessing one of the two coffees I knocked from his hands was for you, then."

"Oh, yes, he told me about that," she said with a knowing smile.

Eliza reached up to swat my shoulder. "You spilled coffee on him? What a good meet-cute."

"Not a meet-cute." I swatted her shoulder in return. "Because you know who saw me afterward? Eddy. In all my stained, laundry-day, unbrushed-hair glory."

"Oh, no." Eliza covered her mouth but continued to laugh.

I narrowed my eyes at her until Aggie released a dramatic sigh, and I turned to find her rolling her eyes.

"At some point, you're either going to have to tell that boy you have feelings or move on, because he is oblivious, child. Absolutely oblivious."

"No, he's just...waiting for the right time, I think." *I hoped.* "Or maybe he doesn't see me in that way. That would be understandable too."

"That wouldn't be understandable at all. You would be the *catch* of the day." Aggie chuckled to herself, taking a seat on a bench along the wall.

"Exactly," Eliza said. "Although, I wouldn't phrase it like that. You are such a kind, loving person, Remi. He would be lucky to have you."

I sat beside her on the attic step with a sigh, propping my chin on my hands. "Maybe I do need to tell him. Maybe he just doesn't realize I'm..."

"Totally in love with him?" Eliza said.

Aggie groaned. "Love? Is that what we're calling it?"

"What would you call it?" I asked.

Aggie smirked, lifting a white brow. "Lust?"

My mouth fell open and snapped shut with a smile. "Oh, shut up, you old coot."

"Old coot? I'll remember that next time you want cider." She stood, smoothing out her velvet dress with a smug expression.

"You don't hold out on the cider, and I won't hold out on the apple fritters."

Her eyes snapped to me, smugness gone. "You wouldn't dare."

"Don't try me."

She shook her head, muttering to herself. "All right, this old coot has got to get home. You two may not need your beauty sleep, but I sure do. I can't wait to see how you do this place up."

"Bye, Aggie," we said in unison.

"Goodnight, children," she said, her beaded bracelets jingling as she waved over her shoulder.

"I'm old enough to be your mother," I shouted as she disappeared down the stairs, but her answering laughter echoed up to us.

4

EARLY BIRD GETS THE FRITTER

The sun kissed the horizon, soft yellow light peeking in through the open kitchen window.

I'd been baking for the last hour or so, sipping a warm coffee when I had time, wearing my favorite attire: my feet cozy in fuzzy socks and the rest of me wound up in my even fuzzier robe.

Being bundled up and listening to nostalgic Halloween music with the windows open to the chilly air made me so content, I could cry. I lived for these kinds of mornings.

There was magic in them, I was sure. A soul-soothing magic, designed specifically for my soul in particular—or at least one mine called for.

"Somebody's Watching Me" started in my headphones, and a smile curved my lips. I took another gulp of coffee and danced to the music, singing along as I tossed a few dishes into the sink. I wiped the counters down and moved the coffee pot to the breakfast table along with the mug tree.

When the oven dinged, the scent of fresh apple fritters permeating the air, I ran and slid across the floor on my socks until I stopped in front of the oven. With my orange mitts, I pulled the baking sheet from the oven, turned to sit it on the island, and screamed.

"Somebody *is* watching me," I muttered under my breath as I sat the tray down on the island and pulled my headphones off.

Jack leaned on the door frame with his arms crossed over his chest and a ridiculous grin on his face.

"Didn't anyone teach you it was wrong to spy?" I asked, pulling the mitts off.

"Was it spying? I wasn't hiding. I was just"—he held his arms out to the side as he strolled to the coffee pot—"waiting for you to see me."

I rolled my eyes. "Well, I saw you, and you'd have sent me into cardiac arrest if my heart still beat."

He grabbed a mug and poured a cup before glancing at me with a cocked brow. "I thought vampires had heightened senses?"

"We do…to an extent." I turned and hopped onto the counter, crossing my legs as I lifted my mug. "But it's been so over-exaggerated. Something human men with fragile egos came up with ages ago to make themselves feel better when they got bested by a woman."

His laughter boomed, and my eyes flicked to him.

"I don't doubt that for a second." He turned and reclined on the counter. "So, you volunteer at Books and Boos, run a B&B, *and* bake? A woman of many talents."

My head tilted ever so slightly, a soft flush burning my cheeks. "And what do you do?"

His gaze dropped to his mug. "I'm a writer."

"Really? What do you write? Anything I would've heard of?"

"I love to write fantasy." His eyes lifted back to me, a

dazed gleam in them. "But no, nothing you've heard of. That's actually why I came back for a visit. My grandma used to tell me all these bedtime stories when I was a kid and that really started my love for it. I was kind of hoping being back here would just..."

"Inspire you?"

He grinned. "Yes, inspire me."

Eliza and Robert walked in then, alongside Fred and our neighbor, Ara—the local energy witch—and her husband, Rogue. He was one of a kind, a bat boy who loved carrying their daughter strapped to his chest, just as she was now. With two large wings, he barely fit through the door.

Jack's eyes were as wide as saucers as he took in Rogue, and I stifled a laugh.

Rogue, however, didn't stifle his laughter at all. It echoed through the kitchen as he stuck a hand out to Jack. "Hey, man. My name is Rogue."

"Jack." He shook Rogue's hand, his gaze still glued to his maroon wings. Jack blinked rapidly and shook his head. "Sorry, I shouldn't stare."

"It's all right." Rogue waved a hand before strolling to the breakfast table and taking a seat. "I get it all the time. Trust me."

Ara quickly introduced herself next and joined her husband, grinning from ear to ear as V reached for a roll.

"Well, hello there. My name is Eliza," she said, beaming. "We didn't get a chance to meet yesterday."

Robert stuck a hand out to Jack next, introducing himself. "Robert."

"Jack." He shook Robert's hand and then Eliza's. "Nice to meet you both."

Fred introduced himself last, as slow as ever, and took his normal seat around the large breakfast table. All the chairs were mismatched and none matched the table, but I loved it. It only added character.

The table sat beneath the largest window in the room—a bay window that framed the sunrise beautifully with pumpkins and sunflowers covering its bench.

"So, Jack, whatcha in town for?" Robert said as he handed a roll to Eliza.

She smiled and glanced at Jack, waiting for his answer—as did the rest of them. *Nosy.*

"Aggie is my grandmother, and she roped me into coming for the month."

"Ah, she can be persuasive." Ara chuckled.

"That she can be," Jack sighed as he grabbed another tray of food and brought it to the table.

"Thanks," I said and handed him another when he turned back to me.

"Welcome." He narrowed his eyes at me but took the tray, sitting it on the table beside the others. "But I haven't been back in years. It was time for a visit."

Painstakingly slowly, Fred reached across to grab the coffee pot and poured himself a steaming cup. "You picked the perfect time to come."

"That's what I keep hearing." Jack peeked at me with a grin.

After that, the conversation ceased—a good sign. It meant the food was good, and I always took it as the highest compliment. Today was no different.

Breakfast went rather quickly, as it normally did before people dispersed to their daily lives, and I made quick work of cleaning up the kitchen before hurrying to my room to get ready for the day. After a shower, I pulled on my favorite black jeans and blood-red tank top before running a brush through my hair. Leaning over the vanity to get a better look in the mirror, I lined my lips with red and darkened my lashes with mascara. Satisfied, I pulled on my Converses and stepped into the hallway.

My room was on the bottom floor, near the stairwell and the front door, so I wasn't entirely surprised when I shut my door and turned to see Jack coming down the stairs.

"Heading to Books and Boos?" I asked as I grabbed my jacket.

"Yep. Care to walk me? I'm not sure I know how to get back." He chuckled, running a hand through his black hair.

"Sure." I opened the door and motioned him out. "I'm going through Shadow Park, though. Up for meeting another Hallow Falls resident?"

"Always." He jogged down the front porch stairs and turned back to extend a hand to me.

"Oh, what a gentleman." I feigned gratitude as I shut the front door and dipped into a faint curtsy before sliding my hand into his with a laugh.

"Well, you seem to have an affinity for falling. I think it would be rude of me not to at least *try* to prevent that."

I jerked my hand back, giving him a flat look, but his eyes shifted to the house and his jaw fell slack.

"Holy...Halloween. You two did an incredible job in just one night."

"Thank you." I smiled and turned with my hands on my hips to admire our work. We had gotten a lot done in a short amount of time, and it was exactly Eliza's vision.

Half of our large yard had become a maze of hay bales while the other half was covered in a pumpkin patch and fake cemetery. The smoke machines were placed and hidden, ready to release their creepy haze. Ghosts hung from every tree and along the corners of the porch with purple and orange lights covering the rails beneath gauzy cobwebs.

We didn't leave an inch to spare. It was packed with happiness and warmth.

"Fred is going to sit with them." I pointed to the fake scarecrow and mummy in the front porch chairs. "That way he can jump and scare the kids when they come up for candy."

"Genius," he said. "This reminds me so much of when I was a kid."

"That's what we were going for: nostalgic."

"Well, you nailed it."

"Thank you," I said and strolled down the front walk.

He took another look before following me. "So, are we going to meet the pumpkinhead guy?"

"Ambercup. He's a good friend of mine. He's nearly as old as me, so we've been together for as long as I can remember."

"Together? Are you two—"

"Friends." I laughed, shaking my head. "We've been friends for forever."

"Ah," he said and slid his hands into his leather jacket pockets. "How old are you, anyway?"

My eyes cut to him with mock offense. "Isn't that supposed to be a rude question to ask?"

"Considering you look a solid twenty-five, I wouldn't think so."

I flicked my hair over my shoulder dramatically at the compliment. "Well, thanks, but I turn 153 this year, actually."

When he stopped, I turned and stifled a laugh at his shocked expression.

"How long do vampires live?" he asked.

"I'm still young, buddy. Stick around long enough and I'll introduce you to Dracula. Now, *he's* old."

"Dracula?" His voice raised an octave. "I assumed he was a story told to scare children."

I suppressed a smile, turning to walk again. He joined me as we strode across the empty street and stepped into Shadow Park. "Well, I'd hope so. He's my grandfather."

"You're kidding."

"Nope. Although, the stories—like most others—are exaggerated." I groaned, rolling my eyes. "Kill a few people and suddenly people think you're a monster."

He stopped again, and I looked over my shoulder. "I'm kidding."

He nodded once. "So, Dracula isn't your grandfather?"

"Oh, no. He is, but he's not a killer. He's actually just your typical sweet old man. He plays shuffleboard, drinks his decaf coffee, and hangs out at the local library. He does love to read the stories humans write about him, though."

"That is so...weird," Jack mumbled, shaking his head.

"Not weird." I nudged him with an elbow. "Nothing should surprise you. Every legend originates from some-where. It may be twisted or enlarged or darkened, but it always has an origin, and a lot of the time, those origins reside right here in Hallow Falls."

He didn't have a chance to reply before Amber came into view, strolling towards us on his spindly legs. He smiled his empty smile, the orange light flickering behind it. "You must be Aggie's grandson."

He stuck out a bony hand, and Jack stared for a beat before sliding his hand into it with a grin. "That'd be me."

5

MOONLIT MOONSHINE

I stepped onto the porch with the last two bowls of candy—the kind with the hand that'll jump out when kids reach in.

Handing them to Eliza, I checked over the rest of the decor.

It was perfect. "Monster Mash" drifted from the speakers, the graveyard shimmered with white haze, and lanterns glowed with small flickering flames. Robert was dressed as a scarecrow, standing at the front of his hay maze while Fred sat in his rocking chair, swaying back and forth as he waited for his first victims.

"This'll be fun." Fred tossed a piece of chocolate in his mouth.

Eliza nodded, beaming as she took a deep breath and looked around.

I darted inside to grab my coat and the basket of baked goods before stepping back onto the porch. Handing Eliza the basket, I quickly pulled my jacket on as she lifted the lid to peek inside.

"Hmm, pumpkin. I hope you saved some for the rest of us."

Winking, I took the basket back. "There are about a dozen pumpkin rolls on the kitchen counter along with a loaf of bread. I wouldn't forget about my favorite ghosts."

"Did you hear that, Rob? We're her favorite," she shouted as she nudged my arm.

"Was there ever any doubt?" he hollered back.

Her face softened as she turned back to me. "No, never."

"I love you, guys." I threw an arm over her shoulders.

"And we love you."

With a sigh and one final glance around, I said, "All right, I'm going to run these to Town Square and check out our competition, but I'll be back later."

"Have fun," she said as I jogged down the front steps. "And maybe find a date to walk through it with, hmm?"

I whipped back around to face her, but she had returned to fidgeting with the cobwebs, a sly grin still visible in her profile.

"Oh, shut up," I chuckled and continued on my way.

A breeze had picked up in the town, creating a chill in the air, but the sky was clear, the moonlight bright as I made it to Books and Boos.

It glowed purple in the middle of Town Square with a dense fog hanging around the massive cauldron placed out front. It'd taken us far too long to carry that thing out this afternoon, both heavy and large; Aggie had filled it with some kind of potion that she said would guarantee her win.

Jack and I had burst into laughter when it turned out to be her apple cider with way too much apple pie moonshine mixed in, but it would absolutely sway the people of Hallow Falls. We were all suckers for her cider.

"Any *potion* for the competition?" I asked as I strolled up to Aggie. "I'll trade you for a pumpkin roll."

She stirred her giant vat, dressed in a dark violet dress and a pointed witch hat. "I suppose."

She grabbed a cup from the table beside her and ladled the cider, pouring me a large paper cup full. After she popped the lid on, she replaced the ladle on the side of the cauldron and handed the cup to me.

I sipped it carefully, and as soon as it hit my tongue, my eyes rolled back. "Are you kidding? This has to be cheating. Its too good."

The liquid slid down my throat and warmed my belly.

She cocked a brow at me. "And strong."

"Yeah, I can tell, and I'll be back for my second cup of liquid courage after I drop these off." I held the basket up. "Speaking of..." I pulled out a wrapped roll for her.

"Ah, yes. Your bribery. And you have the nerve to say *my* cider is cheating."

I snatched the treat back before she could grab it. "Hey, now! I'm not handing them out to the judges."

"Right." She nodded with raised brows.

Chuckling, I handed it to her, and she took it gratefully, unwrapping it while we walked to her nearby bench. As soon as she sat down, Pum jumped up into her lap, but she nudged him back off. "Nope. Not sharing this time."

"Aw, poor guy." I couldn't help but laugh when he huffed and slipped back into the shop.

"Thank you for helping us set up today, by the way," she said, wiping her mouth.

"Of course. You know I love being here."

Jack stepped out then, dressed in black, topped with a leather jacket, and his eyes fell on me. "Do you ever go anywhere else?"

"Watch it," Aggie said before I could respond. "She's my best helper here, and she brought this." She lifted the roll, already half eaten.

I shrugged. "None for you, though. Sorry."

His mouth ticked up as he strolled over, his hands in his pockets. "I'm sure I'll find some at breakfast."

I rolled my eyes and sipped my overly strong cider, reveling in the burn as I turned toward the Square. My gaze roamed over the elated faces and decorated booths. It wasn't long before I found Eddy's, as rugged and happy as ever. When we made eye contact, he waved, and I smiled, my cheeks flushing as I lifted my cup to him.

Aggie sat up and motioned someone over. "Oh, Jack. Come here, child. I have someone for you to meet."

She stood, holding her hand out, and it was Amara who slid her hand into Aggie's. She tugged her over to Jack, his expression confused.

"This is Maggie's granddaughter, Amara. She didn't have anyone to walk with, so I thought my handsome, gentlemanly grandson could do the honors."

Jack blinked once, twice, then cleared his throat and stuck a hand out to her. "Of course. My name is Jack."

"It's nice to meet you," Amara said with a shy smile.

"You'll have to show me around. This is my first Ghost Walk." Jack offered her an elbow.

She slid her arm into his as she said, "I'd be happy to."

Aggie came and sat back beside me with a satisfied gleam in her eyes.

"Did he know you were setting him up?"

"Nope."

I stifled a laugh. "Didn't think so."

"Now, where's yours? Ah, there he goes." She pointed her finger, and it followed Eddy as he walked to the half-empty table of baked goods where the town's cake baker stood, staring directly at me with her hands on her hips.

"Oh, I have to go." I jumped up and darted across the street, Aggie's laughter trailing behind me.

"Come back and get another cup later, dear!" Maggie shouted as she stepped out from Books and Boos.

I waved over my shoulder to her and strode across the lawn to the baker's table, handing the basket to her. "Hey, sorry I'm late."

"No worries." Sara reached in for the wrapped goods and set them onto her expertly decorated displays. "Thank you for bringing these. There's no way I could've filled up this table alone."

"Yeah, thank you for these." Eddy grabbed a roll and one of Sara's cupcakes before handing her a few dollars.

"You're welcome," I said, keeping my eyes on my hands as I handed a few more treats to Sara.

Leaning over the table, he whispered, "And just in case no one has told you yet, you look good tonight, Remi."

My breathing hitched, and I nearly dropped the basket I was moving. I caught it and carefully set it on the table as I glanced up to find him grinning, as cocky and confident as ever.

"Are you drunk?" I asked, laughing the compliment off, even as I desperately wanted him to mean that.

He feigned offense and planted his hands on the table. I stared at them for a moment too long before my eyes crawled up his forearms, bare with his flannel sleeves rolled up around his elbows.

"No, I just have eyes," he said.

Don't be a coward. Biting my lip, I grabbed the cup of cider, downed the last bit of it, and spit the words out before I could second guess myself. "Hey, so I was actually going to ask you something."

He stood upright again and tilted his head to the side, a curious grin curving his lips. "What's up?"

"Well, I—"

"Hey, Ed. You ready?"

My mouth snapped shut as a blonde werewolf joined his side.

He looked down at her, nodding. "Yeah, hold on. I was just talking to Remi real quick."

I shook my head. "Oh, no, it's nothing really. I was just... going to ask if you ever take volunteers at the dog shelter. I would love to, you know, take a few for a walk or something."

He eyed me, his brows furrowing slightly. "Of course. We could always use more hands. Just get back to me on Monday, all right?"

I nodded and gritted my teeth as they walked off, arms linked at the elbow. I sighed, turning away as they disappeared into the crowd, and locked eyes with Jack's piercing blue. He stared for a second before winking and returning his attention to his own date.

"So close, yet so far," Sara whispered beside me.

So close.

After we finished setting up her booth, I grabbed my basket and turned back toward Books and Boos. I took my time strolling over, the disappointment sinking in my gut with each step.

"Well, I had the courage this time." I plopped down on the bench.

Maggie handed me another cup of cider as Aggie sat beside me. "We saw that."

My skin crawled; I could nearly feel their pity. I

squirmed and gulped down the cider as Amber stepped up to the cauldron. He was dressed in a black pinstripe suit, fitted to his spindly figure and highlighting his large pumpkin head, the fire lit within especially bright tonight.

"Hey, there," he said with curious caution. His eyes flicked from me to Aggie and back.

I lifted my cup to him. "I almost asked Eddy to be my date tonight."

"Almost?"

"Well, his date walked over before I had the chance."

"Ah," was all he said.

Maggie handed him his own cup as I finished my second. Amber smiled and stepped over to kneel in front of me, holding his cup up to me as if it were a ring. "Remi, would you do me the highest of honors and walk with me this night?"

I jerked to my feet, feigning happy tears as I clutched my chest. "I could think of no one I would rather spend my night with than you, Ambercup. Yes. Yes, I accept."

He rose to his feet and grabbed my hand, sliding the cup into it. I took a large gulp and stared at him for a split second before we burst into laughter.

6

MAKING A DEAL WITH THE DEVILISHLY HANDSOME WITCH

Amber and I drank enough cider to put down a small horse by the time he walked me back to the Dead and Breakfast, but we were deliriously happy. The Walk had ended an hour or two ago with Aggie being declared the winner.

I wasn't upset about the loss of title, not this time. This year had been a record-breaking year for the organization. An anonymous donor had donated five grand on top of all the purchased voting tickets and booths—a huge win for the entire town.

I walked along the curb, holding my hands out to either side for balance. When I swayed, Amber jerked a hand out to catch me.

"You're a good friend, Amber. Thank you."

"I'm just returning the favor."

I was too focused on my carefully planted steps to see Jack before I heard him. "I can take it from here if you want to head home, Ambercup."

Amber looked to me, and I nodded, releasing his hand. He smiled as he bowed at the waist with his hands out to either side. "Thank you for another spectacular night, Remi."

I stumbled off the curb and dipped into a curtsy. "My pleasure, Mr. Pumpkinhead."

He spun on his heel and walked across the street to his park, whistling a spooky tune.

With a sigh, I turned to face Jack. He held an elbow out, and I slid my arm into his.

"Well, where's your date? Walk her home already?"

"Yeah," was all he said as we strolled up the front walk. "I didn't expect Ambercup to be your date."

"Date is a strong word."

"Ah, and you didn't want to ask Eddy?"

The smile slid from my face. I pulled my arm from his and held onto the handrail as we ascended the steps. "As I'm sure you saw, he already had a date."

"You didn't answer my question."

"I know."

He opened the door and motioned me forward. I stepped in and strode to my room, shucking my coat off. I tossed the it on the bed and jumped when I turned to see Jack standing in my doorway, leaning on the frame.

"Do you want him to notice you?"

I rolled my eyes. My head was too fuzzy for this conversation, the room nearly swaying around me. "What do you mean notice? He knows who I am."

"Are you evading my questions?" He strolled into my room.

I watched him carefully as I leaned back on my dresser, and he plopped down on my bed. He stretched his legs out in front of him, crossing at the ankle, and rested his arms behind his head.

"What are you talking about? What are you even doing here? In case you forgot, you have your own room."

"Did you know my grandmother was going to set me up?"

I laughed and grabbed a makeup wipe. Leaning closer to the mirror, I slid the wipe along my lips to remove the red lipstick. "No, actually. Although, the surprise on your face was quite funny."

"Well, according to Maggie, that's not the only date she has lined up for me. She wants me to 'find love and settle down here.'"

"Okay...and?" I stalked over to my closet and grabbed a T-shirt. Turning away from Jack, I pulled the tank top off, tossed it in the basket, and pulled the giant shirt on before kicking the jeans off.

"I'll ask again. Do you want Eddy to notice you?"

I gasped at how close his voice sounded and turned to find him right behind me. Tilting my face up to him, I mumbled, "I didn't realize you'd gotten up."

"Do you?"

"Yes," I said in a rush. "I want him to notice me."

His smile became devilish, and I took a step back.

"And I don't want any more blind dates," he said.

"What do you want me to do about that?"

"I want you to date me."

A snort escaped, and I covered my mouth. "Yeah, okay."

I walked around him toward the bed, but he slid his hand into mine and swiveled me back to him. "Fake date, obviously."

I paused, my brows furrowing as I considered his words.

"Grandma will get off my back, and I guarantee Eddy

will notice you. Men want the wanted, and I will make sure he knows I want *you* more than any other."

I blinked rapidly, his spicy cologne clouding my already fuzzy mind. I placed a hand on his chest, and his eyes dropped to it as I pushed him back a few steps.

"That is crazy."

He grinned and cocked a dark brow. "Crazy enough to work."

Could it, though?

"Look," he said, stepping closer, "You can date Eddy. Date anyone. I don't care—as long as you're mine in front of Grandma, and we have her thoroughly convinced for the rest of the month."

"We can make Eddy jealous?" I whispered. *Why am I considering this?*

I froze when he placed his hand on my cheek and slowly slid it back so his fingers were in my hair, his palm gripping my jaw as he tilted my face to his.

"Wouldn't you be?" he whispered. "If you were looking at a couple doing this?"

He slid his lips along mine, and my breath hitched. I tugged at his wrist and pulled his hand from my hair.

"No kissing policy."

"What?" He laughed.

"If we're to do this, I want a no kissing policy," I said, flustered.

"On the lips?" he asked with a one-sided grin, revealing a dimple.

I stared at it, suddenly distracted. My brows pulled together as I shook my head, and it swam with the motion. "Of course, not on the lips. What do—"

"Deal." He stuck a hand out.

I looked at it for a moment before sliding my hand in. "Deal."

We shook, and a wave of something grazed over my skin. It almost felt like the tickling magic that solidified deals made with...witches.

Oh, no. My eyes widened slightly. I just made a deal with the grandson of a witch, and he set it in stone.

"Did you just..."

"We have to make it convincing. My grandma will not fall for a flimsy half-assed show."

"Obviously." I rolled my eyes and swayed from the nauseating movement.

He steadied me before leading me to the bed, and I climbed in gratefully.

"All right, then." He pulled the covers up and tucked me in. "Goodnight, Remi."

I swatted his hands away. "Go, and turn the lights off on your way out."

His laughter was the only thing that permeated the dark silence after he left, carrying me into my drunken slumber.

7

THE GREEN-EYED MONSTER IS A WEREWOLF

The pounding in my head was only marginally eased by my second cup of coffee—or was it third?

I didn't have much memory after Amber and I left the Walk, but I did remember having an amazing night, minus the one painfully disappointing moment. It was spent with drinks, friends, good food, and even better Halloween decorations. I couldn't ask for more.

Breakfast barely made it onto the table by the time the sun rose and people trickled into the kitchen. Robert and Eliza found me first, relaying their excitement about the night before. The yard was full of kids coming and going all night, all the pumpkins carved and candy taken.

The neighbors filed in next, their daughter giggling from the carrier on Rogue's chest.

"V loved playing with all the pumpkin guts last night," Ara said, smiling as she handed her daughter a sliced strawberry. "So slimy, huh?" she cooed to her while Rogue watched on with a sweet smile curving his lips.

We all sat around the table as Fred and Jack joined us.

Throwing a quick glance in their direction, I reached over to grab a honeyed biscuit and said, "Morning."

"Morning," Jack drawled, sliding his hand over my shoulders.

I stilled, my eyes wide as I stared at the tray in front of me. I blinked once and lifted my gaze to Eliza whose eyes were just as wide, her smile curious.

"Uh...hi." I turned to him as he sat in the chair next to me.

"So, where's the pumpkin rolls? I *know* you left some here last night."

Robert grabbed a roll from the counter behind him and tossed it at Jack. He laughed, catching it mid-air, and took a bite. When he moaned dramatically, I rolled my eyes, fighting a smile.

"They taste as good as they look." He bumped me with his shoulder and lowered his voice to whisper, "I'm sure *other things* do as well."

The smile slid from my face. My cheeks warmed, but I didn't look at him. Instead, I shoved another bite of fruit in my mouth and pretended I didn't hear him at all. There was no way he meant to say that...or meant it in the way I heard it.

No way.

I STROLLED past Shadow Park on my way to the coffee shop when I heard Jack's voice call my name.

I slowed, glancing over my shoulder as he jogged to my side.

"Where ya heading?" he asked.

"To get another coffee," I replied. "Hey, about this morning...what was that?"

"We put on a pretty good show, hmm?"

"Show?" I stopped walking.

He paused, raising a brow. "You don't remember?"

"Remember what?"

His eyes roamed over my face for a moment before he released a low chuckle and took a step toward me to grab my hand. He held my wrist up, and I swallowed hard, resisting the urge to pull my hand back as his fingers grazed over my skin.

He slid my sleeve back to reveal the mark.

"Oh, Ghouls." My head fell to my palm as the bits and pieces of the night before started to trickle in—images of Jack in my room, dangerously close, touching me... "Did we?"

"Did we what?" he asked before understanding dawned on him, his lips curving into a devious smile. "Did we fuck? No, unfortunately not."

His laughter grated my already frayed nerves, and I realized he was still holding my wrist. I jerked my hand free and raised it to my face to examine it. Wrapped around the base of my wrist was a thorny, black vine—my shackle. Each witch's shackle mark was different, but they were always marked into the skin when a deal was struck and the witch found the person untrustworthy.

To be marked was to guarantee the deal would be carried out.

My eyes cut to him. "I thought you were human...mostly."

"I am *mostly*, but my grandmother's bloodline is strong, so some magic has trickled down—bargainer's magic being one of them."

I took a deep breath, throwing my hands out to the side. "All right, I remember making a deal...kind of, but I don't remember what I agreed to."

He laughed, sliding an arm through mine, and tugged me forward. "You, my little monster, are to be my date for the month."

"No." I pulled my arm from his. "No, I wouldn't have agreed to that."

"Are you sure?"

"I'm not going to date you, Jack." I chuckled nervously as the shackle tingled on my wrist. "I already have feelings for someone else."

"Eddy?" He cocked a brow.

My eyes narrowed as I glared at him, my thoughts racing. "Were you eavesdropping on me?"

"No, Remi, I wasn't eavesdropping," Jack said. "That was part of our deal. Together, we're going to get Grandma off me and get Eddy under you."

I slapped a hand over his mouth and glanced around, my cheeks burning. "Jack!"

He smiled beneath my palm and grabbed my wrist, pulling it from his face to hold it next to his, revealing his matching bracelet of thorns. "No going back now."

I groaned; we were locked in. The deal must be upheld, or these marks would burn into our skin and become permanent for the rest of the world to see—the traditional sign of dishonesty. As it was now, only he and I could see them, and I would make damn sure it stayed that way.

Dropping my head to my hand, I rubbed my pounding forehead. "I need a coffee...an Irish coffee."

I started toward the coffee shop again, and Jack jogged to my side.

"I get it. Hair of the dog and all."

My face whipped to him, irritation pricking at my already aching skull. We were mere inches from each other, but I couldn't be bothered. "Why me, of all people? Why did you have to do this"—I held my marked wrist up—"to me?"

"Look, if Aggie is going to force me to date someone this entire month, I'd rather at least like who I'm looking at."

Aggie. I sighed and scrunched my eyes.

This was growing more convoluted by the minute. I couldn't imagine deceiving her, but based on our matching marks, I didn't have a choice. Not unless I wanted to live the rest of my days with Jack's thorny shackle inked on my wrist for everyone to see.

"And like I said last night, you can date Eddy or whoever, whenever," he said, running a hand through his dark hair. "As long as you're mine in front of Grandma and we pull this off, nothing else matters. Not to me, anyway."

"Why don't you just leave? Why go through with all this at all?"

He looked at me like I'd asked him a question he hadn't already considered. "I haven't been here since I was a kid, and I just want to spend a Halloween here, where my family is from. I want to experience everything Grandma has been raving about all these years." He slid his hands into his pockets and laughed. "I just don't want to date a bunch of random people while I'm at it."

I nodded slowly. "Why did you mark me, though? You don't trust me?"

"I didn't want you to change your mind." He shrugged as if it was no big deal. As if I wasn't *marked*. Maybe it didn't mean anything to him, but it did to me. "Besides, I kind of like the thought of you wearing my mark. It's like our own little secret, hmm?"

My mouth opened to respond, but no words would form. What was I supposed to say to that?

His gaze dropped to my lips, that dimple appearing in his cheek when he grinned and raised a hand to my face. I froze as he tucked a strand of hair behind my ear before sliding his fingers beneath my chin. When he tilted my face up to him, something stuttered in my chest.

"Don't worry, Remi." His eyes dropped to my mouth. "They'll both disappear when I leave in November."

When did he get so close?

He leaned closer, his lips nearly skimming mine, and I pulled back an inch.

My first kiss was not going to be with someone like this, in a situation like this. It was saved for—

"Remi?" Eddy said from behind me.

Jack smiled, and a subtle flick of his eyes told me he already knew Eddy was headed toward us.

"Oh, hey," I said, turning nonchalantly as I screamed on the inside.

Jack slid an arm around my waist, and I leaned into his side, his body warm and scent as spicy as ever.

Eddy's eyes slid from me to Jack and back. "I know you mentioned wanting to volunteer at the shelter last night, and I thought we could grab coffee and talk about it?"

Finally! I opened my mouth to answer, but Jack spoke first.

"Aw, sorry, man. She's actually booked for the day." My eyes cut to him with frustration, and he squeezed my waist as he pulled me into him. My body was flush with his, and I fought the urge to pull away. "Guess I beat you to it, huh, Ed?"

Eddy cleared his throat, and I blinked rapidly before

pulling my gaze away from Jack's face. "All right. Another time, then?"

Jack led me forward, and as we passed, I let my hand graze over Eddy's arm. His eyes flicked to where I touched him, following the movement.

"I would love to grab coffee another time, though." I waved over my shoulder without so much as a glance back. "See ya, Eddy."

"See you, Remi."

As soon as we rounded the corner out of Eddy's sight, I slid from Jack's grip, beaming. "Okay, I'm in."

Jack shook his head as he pulled the coffee shop door open and motioned me in. "Good, because it's not only him we have to convince."

8

THE MAIZE MAZE

Tonight was the first night of many in which we would have to convince the town *and* Aggie that we were together.

I rubbed my palms together nervously, breathing hot air onto my freezing hands before Jack cupped them between his gloved ones and pulled me closer.

"It'll be fine. We don't have to be in love," he said. "We just met, and she knows that. It's casual, Remi. Just be casual."

"I'm trying, but it's Aggie. She's known me for decades. Not to mention, she has...senses. She'll know we're lying."

His mouth ticked up in a smirk before his eyes landed on something—or someone—behind me. "Then don't lie. You *are* my date, Remi. Nothing more, nothing less."

He slid around me, taking my hand, and I swiveled to find Aggie and Maggie strolling toward us. Aggie's eyes slid to our conjoined hands before I even had the chance to smile in greeting.

"Well, what do we have here?" Maggie drawled.

"It's just a date." Jack squeezed my hand once, as if the

words were meant more for me than them, and let me go to throw an arm around his grandmother's shoulders. A ridiculous grin stretched across his face as they *both* stared at me. "Don't make a big deal about it, all right?"

"All right," Aggie agreed, but a smug curiosity swirled behind her eyes.

Why did I feel suddenly feel flayed open and on display? I was pretty sure Aggie couldn't read minds—well, maybe seventy five percent sure—yet my skin crawled beneath the weight of their gazes. Although, in a shocking turn of events, it wasn't Aggie's that had me shifting on my feet.

It was *his*.

At least I knew Aggie. She was kind and honest, a girl's girl, but Jack? I didn't know him at all. Aggie simply looked for truth while he stared for an entirely different reason, one I wasn't aware of, but his gaze felt predatory, and like the prey I *wasn't*, I had the sudden urge to run and hide.

I blinked rapidly when the shackle encircling my wrist started to burn. With a hard swallow, I forced a smile on my face and shrugged, hoping the darkness would be enough to hide my growing flush, but even I knew that was wishful thinking.

Jack *finally* ended my torture, releasing Aggie as he tipped his head to the maze. "Well, are we ready?" When Aggie and Maggie nodded, he gestured to the entrance. "Ladies first."

They started forward, and I stepped to follow, but Jack slipped an arm around my waist, lowering his mouth dangerously close to my ear. I nearly felt his words as he whispered, "Nice touch with the blush."

My steps stuttered, but the moment ended as quickly as it began. He released me, and I haphazardly sucked in a breath, glaring at the back of his head as he walked ahead to join Aggie.

WHILE ALL FOUR of us entered the haunted corn maze together, Jack and I had split from them not long after we started. He insisted we go left while Aggie and Maggie laughed, waving over their shoulders as they strolled to the right without another glance back.

I regretted following Jack *deeply*, but considering our... predicament, we were better for it. We could relax without Aggie's questioning gaze. Unfortunately for us, however, Aggie seemed to be the only one of us with any directional sense.

I knew it was a complicated maze this year, but as we neared the end of an hour lost within its confines, I started to contemplate walking straight through the corn.

When we took a turn and stared at *another* dead end, I released an exasperated sigh and dropped my head back to stare at the night sky. "We're lost."

"Oh, really?" Jack turned and strode in the opposite direction. "I had no idea."

The dim lighting didn't help either. We couldn't see the moon as it was conveniently tucked behind dense cloud cover, leaving the flickering torches as the only source of light, and the air was chilled, the breeze icy.

"Okay, we have to be at the back." I looked up and down the path—not a single person to be found. "We haven't seen anyone else in at least half an hour. Are we dumb or is everyone else just really good at mazes?"

His feet paused as he released a bark of laughter. "I'm choosing to believe everyone else cheated."

"They had to have," I said. "Okay, let's try this way."

"Lead on." He motioned, and I started to the right.

I took a few steps when I realized I didn't hear him behind me. Turning, I found a wall of corn, but I had just come from that way. I reached a shaking hand out and flinched when I touched the stalks. A wall had formed between us. They were changing.

Adrenaline spiked in my veins.

I never walked the maze alone. Ever.

I reached my hand out and felt the leaves. "Jack?"

He didn't answer. I glanced behind me down the path —empty.

"Jack?" I shouted a bit louder. I could've sworn the sound nearly echoed.

When there was no response, I jogged down the path and darted around the corner. I followed the trail, taking turn after turn, but it was dark, cold, and utterly *empty*.

Memories flashed behind my eyes, blurring reality: bloodied pitchforks and axes, being chased and fleeing for my life, stumbling and sobbing through the forest. The terror of being truly lost freed the panic in my chest.

My feet came to an abrupt halt when air started to evade me.

I stopped and dropped my face to my hands, counting back from ten as I inhaled deeply.

It's just a haunted maze.

I wiggled my toes in my boots, firmly secure on the ground.

Just a maze.

Taking another slow breath, I reached out to the corn stalks. I felt the breeze slide along my cheeks and the cool leaves beneath my fingertips. I focused, listening for the sound of people. When distant laughter and shuffling foot-steps reached me, my breath returned.

You're not lost. You're not alone. You're in Hallow Falls. Aggie and Jack are somewhere close by.

When I had settled some, I lifted my eyes and continued forward, slowly this time. Each step was a choice. I wouldn't let fear control any aspect of my life, not even something as minuscule as my pace.

As I rounded the next turn, I bumped into a solid chest.

"Well, fancy seeing you here," Eddy said. It had been almost a week since Jack and I had last seen him, and his beard was longer, framing his smile.

I exhaled. "Oh, thank Ghouls. I didn't realize the walls were changing."

His brows furrowed. "Changing?" He glanced back, pausing at the wall that had formed behind him. "I hadn't realized either."

"I guess we found what the haunted part was."

He extended a hand forward, and we strolled down the path together. "So, you and Jack?"

"Oh, it's casual. We're just seeing how things go."

"Ah," he replied. "So, about that coffee—"

Jack stepped from the darkness in front of us, jogging down the path. He was paler than usual. "There you are. That was a bit...terrifying." His eyes flicked to Eddy, and he steadied, stifling a grin. "Thanks for finding her for me, Ed. What a gentleman."

"Seems the maze was leading her to me, pal. I can walk her from here."

My gaze shot to Eddy, stunned. I bit my lip against the smile blooming as I turned back to Jack, and he lifted a brow in question.

"I'll meet you at the Dead and Breakfast, okay?" I said.

Jack stuffed his hands in his jacket pockets as he walked past us, his blue eyes locked on mine. "As you wish, little monster," he whispered with a wink.

Eddy let out a long, slow breath. "And he's staying with you?"

"Yeah," I said, glancing up at him before the gravity of that statement hit me. "Oh, no. I mean, yes, at the B&B. Aggie booked him a room. He's her grandson."

"Ah, that makes so much sense. They smell similar."

"Smell?"

He smiled, his warm brown eyes shifted to amber in the flickering firelight. Our steps slowed as he studied my face, but just when I thought he might say something worth hearing, a stiff wind blew through the maze.

I gasped, tightening my arms around myself. He pulled his fleece flannel off without hesitation and wrapped it around my shoulders. His hands hesitated on me for a moment, the warmth from his palms permeating through the fabric. Werewolves always ran hotter than the rest of us, and the feeling was delicious, especially in this cold.

With a sigh, he swiveled me toward the path, guiding me forward with his hand on my lower back. "Yes, smell. Werewolves can smell bloodlines."

"What do I smell like?" The words left my mouth before I could stop them, and my cheeks burned. "Is that a weird question? You don't have to answer that."

"You smell like..." He leaned in close enough that I could feel his breath on the hollow of my throat, and I froze, barely managing not to trip over my own feet. "Cinnamon, if you were to put it in an evergreen forest."

I swallowed hard as he pulled back, putting space between us again.

"And no, it's not weird," he said, tucking my hair behind my ear. "It's nice, actually."

"You smell like firewood," I said, and he cocked his head to the side. "I can't smell bloodlines per se, but I can smell... blood. You smell like you would taste like a roasted marshmallow, fresh off the flames."

"Cinnamon, forests, fires, and marshmallows." He threw an arm over my shoulders and pulled me into his side as we continued down the path. "I'd say that's a damned good combination."

If my heart still beat, it would be hammering against my chest right now. I'd known this man for a decade, yet we'd never been this close.

"So, the other night, the blonde woman..."

"Oh, Natalie?" he asked.

"Uh, sure, Natalie. She was pretty." I scrunched my eyes before asking, "Was she your...date?"

"Yeah, that was our first date, I suppose." His laughter boomed. "Our only date. We didn't really hit it off."

I released a nervous chuckle, nodding. "Ah, okay."

His steps slowed. "Why?"

My mouth pressed into a firm line as I refrained from showing my internal panic. Waving a hand, I said as nonchalantly as possible, "Oh, it's nothing, honestly. I was just... I was going to ask you to walk with me, but Amber stepped in, all white knight style."

"Oh." He ran his hand through his hair. "Well, for the record, I would have walked with you, had I known you wanted to."

"Yeah?"

Am I breathing? The feeling in my chest was overwhelming, and my head was spinning.

"Of course," he said as he extended an elbow. "Walk with me now?"

I smiled and slid my arm through his, reveling in his warmth, but he shook his head when his eyes landed on something behind me. He released a low chuckle, pointing a finger, and I turned to see the exit.

I playfully nudged his side with my elbow while cursing the fates in my head. "I guess we won't be walking far."

"I guess not. Another time, then?"

With a voice much steadier than I felt, I asked, "When we get those coffees?"

Jack appeared then, before Eddy had the chance to answer, and I wanted to wring his neck. He was close.

Too close.

I felt the energy shift in Eddy, but the expression on Jack's face caught my attention. He lifted a dark brow and tilted his head to the side. I looked past him and found Aggie, speaking with the town mayor a few feet from the exit.

"Aggie is waiting on us," he said. "She wants to walk back together."

"Oh."

His eyes were rich with humor as he dipped his head, and the mark on my wrist tingled.

Oh.

"Right." I slid my arm from Eddy's and faced him. "I'll see you another time, okay? Coffee. Very soon."

He smiled and said goodbye, but I felt his gaze on our backs as I exited the maze on Jack's arm.

9

SLEEPLESS IN HALLOW FALLS

Aggie's eyes found us as soon as we exited. "Good Ghouls, did you two get lost in there or what?"

"Well, it is a maze," I replied. "We should've stuck with you two."

"Apparently, we're directionally challenged," Jack added.

Aggie laughed as she pulled her velvet overcoat tighter. "You know what, I'm not surprised in the slightest. Did you like those changing paths, though? Not my idea, but I was excited when Maizy asked me to enchant it."

Maizy was the scarecrow who ran the maze every year, but she had never done anything like this before. I glanced around, looking for her, and she just happened to be walking by. I reached out and swatted her arm.

Her face swiveled to us, but when she realized it was me, she cracked a smile.

"You couldn't warn us?" I asked.

"What fun would that be?" She winked before glancing at Jack. "Well, hello there. I'm Maizy."

She extended a wooden hand, her straw sticking out beneath her flannel sleeves.

"Jack," he said as he shook her hand. "That's quite a maze you have there."

"Well, thank you," she said. "You must be Aggie's grandson. She told me he was overly attractive."

My hand flew to my mouth, covering my grin as I stifled a laugh. I peeked at Jack, and a shocked giggle slipped past my lips when I found his cheeks tinted pink.

"That'd be me," Jack said, throwing a forced smile at his grandmother.

"Yes, it would." Maizy took a step back and let her eyes slide over his form, but before she could continue her perusal, her daughter ran up, half my height and twice as cute. Her red string hair was tied in pigtails, bouncing as she jumped and reached up for her mom.

Maizy leaned over and scooped her up, resting her on her hip. "I guess I should go get this youngin' a donut. See you guys later?"

"Of course," Aggie said and leaned in. "Get this cutie two. She deserves it."

"Really?" her daughter asked excitedly.

Maizy sighed dramatically, but her smile was wide and eyes adoring. "I guess."

Her daughter squealed as they strode off.

"You two did seem to take longer than most, though," Aggie said, and her form shook with laughter. "The maze must have had an agenda."

Jack's smile slid from his face as he turned to his grandmother. "We got separated by those walls. The maze was quite nightmarish without company."

Aggie's face fell slightly, her eyes flashing between the two of us. "Oh, I'm sorry."

I studied Jack, remembering how ashen he was when he found us, and couldn't help but wonder if he shared a similar fear. His gaze was somewhat distant even now.

"We found each other, though, right?" I slid my hand into his and squeezed.

His icy eyes regained a bit of warmth as they lowered to mine. "Right. No harm, no foul, I suppose."

"Right," I repeated, although I wasn't sure I believed it.

SLEEP WAS EVASIVE.

With a frustrated groan, I climbed out of bed and strode to the door, cracking it open to peek my head out. The hallway was empty and quiet, so I padded out, thankful for the fuzzy socks dampening the sound of my footsteps. After grabbing the blanket from the back of the couch, I snuck out the front door and sat on the steps.

The wood was cold beneath me and the icy wind kissed my cheeks, sucking the breath from my chest. Rain fell in sheets, the sound and scent permeating the chilled air. It was beautiful—midnight October rain. It narrowly missed the front steps as the porch was protected by the overhang.

I jumped when the door opened behind me and glanced back to find Jack coming out. Sighing, I turned forward and tightened the blanket around me.

"What are you doing out here?" I asked, a bit disappointed at the loss of isolation. Night storms were meant to be experienced in solitude. They were for reflection and thought and appreciation.

His presence would never allow for that. He was much too distracting.

"Couldn't sleep. Mind if I sit?"

He waited for my nod before taking a seat next to me.

"What's on your mind?" he asked.

"Nothing." I paused, closing my eyes. "Everything. What about you?"

"The same."

Minutes passed with nothing but the whisper of rain between us. There was no expectation, no idle conversation, no awkward silence. It was almost...nice.

When the rain slowed, he finally said, "The maze. It's stupid, but I don't like being alone in the darkness."

"Afraid of the dark?" I chuckled.

"Afraid of what the darkness does." His words confused me, but they were heavy.

"Not everything that lurks in the dark is out to get you," I whispered, the knot in my gut uncomfortable.

He glanced at me before dropping his eyes and letting out a breathy laugh. "No, not everything."

"I was scared, too, you know."

When his eyes flashed back up to meet mine, I paused. His gaze was intense, searing with a mixture of apprehension and...hope?

"Not because of the dark." I swallowed hard and looked away from him to watch the faint trickle falling from the sky. Mist started to form along the yard, clinging to ground in thick clouds. "I don't like being lost—lost and alone."

"Aren't we just two wonderfully fucked up beings?"

I scoffed but couldn't stop the laughter that escaped me. "You'd think the maze would've sensed that. It should've known better than to separate the two scaredy cats."

"Hmm, no," he said. "I wouldn't say we were scaredy

cats. We entered the maze, we managed, and we came out the other side intact. I'd say we were rather—"

"Do *not* say brave." I scrunched my eyes, shaking my head.

"Brave." He nudged me with his shoulder.

I rolled my eyes, but maybe he was right. Or at least it felt better to think about it like that. Anything felt better than being that terrified twenty-year-old again.

And then, for some unfathomable reason, the story tumbled from my mouth. "When I was younger, I tried living in the human world. This was way before your time, back in 1890."

He remained quiet, his face turned to the rain. It felt like he offered me a strange form of privacy by looking away as I spilled the deepest bits of my core to a near stranger, and I was grateful for it.

"They found out what I was, so they created a hunting party. A literal party. They invited me to dinner and after everyone had eaten, the real 'fun' began." I flinched, tightening the blanket around me. I'd never told anyone other than Aggie about this; I didn't know why I was telling it now, to Jack of all people. "They chased me through the forest, and I was utterly...alone. And terrified. They didn't know how to kill a vampire, though. Idiots." I released a low chuckle, but it wasn't humorous.

Jack lifted his hand and rested it on the blanket above mine as I absentmindedly rubbed at his shackle mark on my wrist. His chest rose and fell steadily with each breath, and I let the sound guide my own.

"Grandma doesn't know this—she never will—but the darkness calls to me, to my magic. It beckons me, whispering temptations and promises, and I hate it. I don't want to be twisted into dark magic. That's why I left Hallow Falls years ago and never returned. Out there, magic isn't every-where. Only in certain spots, and they're easy to avoid."

Aggie practiced light magic. It thrived in the sunlight and among the living, based in love and kindness. Dark magic was entirely the opposite. It thrived beneath the moon with the dead. It beckoned lust and depravity.

"Then...why did you come back?" I couldn't imagine any scenario in which I would return to where I was hunted. It wasn't entirely the same situation, but fear was fear. We felt it all the same.

"Well, Grandma really wanted to see me. She's been begging me to visit for years, and I really am a writer. I do want inspiration again." His hand squeezed mine before letting it fall to his lap. "And Hallow Falls is overflowing with it."

"You know what? Fuck the fear," I whispered, feeling a bit ridiculous as I did. "I mean it. I've spent over a century trying and mostly failing to not let it control me, but I'm saying it now. Fuck. The. Fear."

He nodded, his lopsided grin reappearing, accompanied by that damned dimple. "Fuck the fear."

"Those idiots are long dead. I can't lie, I made sure of that. And while I don't know what it feels like for you, I can say for certainty that the magic you choose is exactly that: your choice."

I rested a hand on his shoulder for a moment before sighing and rising to my feet. The rain had stopped, and the air was still. A beam of moonlight shone through the dissi-pating clouds, falling directly over us.

"But just for the record, I know both light and dark witches. The magic doesn't change who you are, and from what I've seen and heard, you are good, Jack."

His lips parted slightly, the silver moonlight illuminating his icy eyes. They were so light, they appeared nearly white—beautifully eerie.

I couldn't deny that even his looks thrived beneath the moon.

"Thank you," he breathed.

I cleared my throat and pulled the blanket off to hand to him. His eyes fell to my bare shoulders, following the thin straps of my tank top lower, lower...

I didn't stop him.

Why didn't I stop him?

His eyes roamed over my form and passed below my flannel pajama shorts down to my fuzzy socks before climbing back to where my hand still held out the blanket. Slowly, he reached up and took it as he met my gaze.

"Goodnight, little monster," he whispered, his smile devilish. He wrapped it around his shoulders as the breeze blew over the porch.

It was cold, and he could tell I wasn't wearing a bra, but his gaze didn't break from mine. He didn't dare lower his eyes to my hardening nipples beneath the thin silk.

No, he simply held my gaze with that same unwavering smirk.

I was suddenly warm. Too warm.

"Goodnight." I nodded once and swiveled on my heel before either of us could say or do anything else.

10

COFFEE ISN'T THE ONLY THING WARM IN HERE

O ctober was passing by too fast for my liking. We'd already blown through the middle of the month.

I exhaled a deep breath, the puff of white steam swirling through the falling drops.

Today was gloomy but comforting. Rain drizzled, pattering off my black umbrella as I strolled to the coffee shop. There hadn't been a break in the clouds in days, but Hallow Falls was beautiful in the dim haziness—the trees especially. While the leaves grew more orange with each dropping degree, the bark was soaked from the rain, painting them a dark black-brown, contrasting perfectly.

These were the trees artists should paint—or at least I would, had I any talent whatsoever with a paintbrush.

The weather had seemed to do Jack some good, too. He'd spent days holed up in the sunroom of the Dead and Breakfast, writing. Each time I passed him, his nose was stuck in either a book, a journal, or a laptop, but never free. Inspiration had struck, and it was consuming his every waking thought.

Not that I minded.

We didn't have to pretend to be into each other when no one was around to see it, and with him so lost in his words, he barely left the house.

While he secluded himself, I still went to see Aggie per usual. I was hesitant at first, but she, shockingly, hadn't pried into us too much. Her curiosity was limited to a few questions but ultimately, she claimed she "wasn't surprised in the slightest that we'd taken to each other." The statement left me a bit confused, but I just nodded wordlessly, and we moved on.

I had left her only moments ago to come here. As I stepped under the overhang, I shook out my umbrella and closed it before pulling the door open. The bell jingled overhead as I stepped inside, glancing left and right.

Eddy sat in the corner beneath a large window, watching the rain fall, holding a mug that appeared entirely too small in his large hands.

As much as I wanted to go sit in that free chair across from him, he wasn't who I was here to see. Unfortunately, today was the day Jack decided to crawl out of his writing cave and ask me to meet him here.

Okay, I almost feel mean for saying unfortunately. Jack's presence was not unfortunate. It was complicated and inconvenient, with the world's worst timing, but not unfortunate.

I glanced around one more time and smiled to myself. Jack wasn't here yet, but Eddy was. His gaze found mine, and he tilted his head, gesturing to the seat in front of him. I started to take a step toward him when the door opened behind me, the bell's jingle cutting through the chatter of the shop.

He didn't have to say a word. I knew it was him. My

wrist tingled, reminding me of my deal, but his scent would have told me either way. It was too distinct; it stood out to me among any other.

"Hello, Remi." Jack snaked an arm around my waist and pulled me into his side, casually kissing the top of my head.

Eddy's chest rose and fell slowly, his mouth pressed into a flat line. I mouthed, "Another time," and he nodded once, turning back to his window.

"What do you want?" Jack asked as he studied the menu hanging behind the counter.

My eyes remained on Eddy as I responded, "Just a chai."

"Is that all?"

"Yep," I sighed.

"Liar," he whispered, low enough for only me to hear.

I swiveled to him, my brows furrowed. "What are you talking about?"

"Nothing," he said, but his smirk said otherwise.

Irritation pricked at me, but he wasn't wrong. A silly little chai was not all I wanted.

He took the cups from the barista and handed me mine.

Following him to a free table, I asked, "Well, how's your story coming along?"

He pulled out a chair and motioned for me to sit. I lifted a brow at him but did so, and he gave me an approving nod before sitting in the chair closest to me rather than across the table.

"Better than it has in a long time."

"Oh, that's good. I guess Hallow Falls was the right call after all, hmm?"

He sipped his coffee, peering over his cup at me before his lips curved up in a smirk. With his free hand, he leaned over to hook his fingers beneath my seat, and in one smooth motion, he pulled my chair closer to him until my knee hit his.

"It would seem so." He took another long sip of his black coffee and reclined in his seat, crossing one ankle over his knee as he threw an arm around the back of my chair.

I blinked once. "Was I not close enough for you?"

He chuckled and leaned down to my ear. "You're never close enough."

"Ah," was all I could manage. I lifted the chai to my lips to busy my mouth before any babbling nonsense could escape and silently prayed he couldn't see the heat rising in my cheeks.

He laughed as he reclined again, and I took a breath, albeit a shaky one. *Who is this man?*

"Poor ole Ed is trying so damn hard to not look this way, but he just can't help himself, can he?"

I fought the urge to look over my shoulder in his direction. "Is that right?"

Jack's smile turned smug as he twisted a strand of my hair around his fingers absentmindedly—or at least appearing to do it absentmindedly. I had a feeling there wasn't a single thing he did that wasn't intended or calculated.

But I also couldn't deny that I liked it. Maybe even loved it. I wanted Eddy to want me, and after a decade of pining, it served him right to be a little jealous.

I rested a hand on Jack's knee, and his twirling paused for a moment before resuming.

"What did you want to meet here for?" I asked, peering through my lashes at him as I took another sip.

His gaze roamed over my face. "Ah, she plays."

"I win," I whispered.

He leaned closer and placed his hand on top of mine,

moving it higher on his thigh. My smile faltered slightly. "I didn't take you for the competitive type."

"You don't know me."

"I'm beginning to."

My gaze fell to his mouth, and he cocked a one-sided smile, revealing his dimple. My lips parted slightly as I got the sudden urge to kiss it.

Clearing my throat, I slid my hand from under his and sat back in my seat.

He groaned quietly. "Temptress."

"You being tempted does not make me the temptress."

"I think that's exactly what it means." My eyes cut to him to find his expression intense, his blue eyes piercing. "Even if it's not intentional."

I swallowed. "Why did you want to meet here?"

"Besides upholding our ruse? I just wanted to get out of the house and get a good cup of coffee."

I sat my mug on the table and sat straighter. "Are you saying my coffee isn't good?"

His laughter echoed through the shop and pulled my own laugh from me.

"Unfortunately, that is what I'm saying."

I scoffed, feigning offense, and swatted his chest, but he caught my hand and pulled me forward. I tumbled into his lap with a gasp, my hands landing on his waist, and he slid a finger beneath my chin, tilting my face to his, stopping just before our lips touched.

My chest rose and fell quickly, but I didn't pull back. I didn't move at all.

I wasn't even sure I wanted to. Something held me here: his smell, his touch, the dimple that sank into his cheek when he realized I wasn't moving.

"Are you sure you want a no kissing policy?" he breathed.

"I-I'm sure." I still didn't move an inch.

His smile deepened. "If you say so."

His eyes flicked down to my mouth and back up before he released me, yet I hovered for a moment, and his grin wavered.

I almost wanted to close the gap. It was just a few inches. Less than a few, actually. Just one.

One measly inch.

His lips were one inch away, and that suddenly felt like a mile, much too far but oh so easily crossed...

The bell jingled again, and my eyes widened, flitting up to meet his.

He leaned down, closing *most* of that damned inch for me, and his words nearly skimmed over my lips as he whispered, "Keep your eyes on the prize, little monster."

I tilted my head to the side, stifling every absurd urge. "I could say the same for you."

"Oh, believe me. I am." His words slid over me like tangible shadows. I could nearly feel them graze along my skin, over my arms, my neck, down my spine...

I practically fell back into my own chair and retrieved my mug, if only to prevent that from happening again.

What is happening to me?

II

SPIRIT HALLOWEEN

Jack was a disease, I'd decided. Not a malicious one but definitely infectious.

The kind that affected the brain...among other things. Our coffee shop interaction was at the forefront of my mind all day, and I'd resorted to stress baking. The kitchen counters were chock full of muffins of every flavor imaginable, but I still felt the need to continue as if the next batch may finally distract me.

His bargainer's magic must be forcing me to focus on it, as I could think of nothing else.

I sighed as I slid the next tray into the oven and turned to recline on the counter, pulling my oven mitts off. I closed my eyes and took a deep breath, inhaling the scent of pumpkins, apples, and cinnamon.

The sound of footsteps caught my attention, and I opened my eyes to find Eddy in the doorway with his hands in his pockets. He smiled sheepishly as he strolled into the kitchen, his eyes roaming over the multitude of baked goods before they found me, his brow arched.

"Stress baking." I shrugged and pushed off the counter to walk over to the kitchen island.

As I leaned onto my elbows across from him, he mirrored me, leaning forward on his hands, and a distracting warmth flowed through me.

"What are you stressed about?" he asked.

My eyes widened before falling to my hands. There was no way in any hell I would say *those* words aloud, not to Eddy, not to anyone. "Just normal things. The B&B, getting everything ready for Halloween, the—"

I stopped abruptly when he slid a hand beneath my chin, tilting my face up to him, and my breath stuttered.

"Let me take you out tonight."

Words wouldn't form. I stared at him, my lips slack.

Say something.

He raised a brow and smiled.

Say something, you idiot.

"Is that a no...?" He tilted his head to the side and chuckled.

"No." I shook my head and cleared my throat. "No, I mean yes. Where to?"

I cringed internally but refused to let him see it.

"I was thinking... Screw the coffee. Since we can't seem to make it there together, how about Benny's?"

Smiling, I bit my lip and nodded. He wanted to take me to Benny's. That was a bar, which meant this was most definitely a date. If he weren't standing directly in front of me, I would've screamed.

"I think the stress is getting to your head." He laughed and tilted my face to him again. I giggled as he shifted my face left and right like he were examining my mind. "You're a bit distracted today."

"You have no idea." I rolled my eyes.

"Well." He pushed off the island and stood straighter, sliding his hands back into his pockets. "Meet me there at eight?"

"Sure," I said nonchalantly and waved.

He walked out of the kitchen, but popped his head back around the corner to add, "Oh, and tonight is their costume party, so wear something...nice."

Then he winked and left.

I stared at the doorway long after he was gone. He just winked at me. Eddy winked at me, and he wanted me to wear something nice.

Good Ghouls, I'm going to pass out.

At the sound of the front door closing, I released my pent-up excitement, squeezing my eyes as I squealed and shimmied.

When I opened them again, Jack had taken Eddy's place in the doorway with his shoulder reclined on the door frame and his arms crossed over his chest—his *bare* chest. I paused as my eyes dipped.

He wasn't wearing a shirt, just gray sweatpants.

Gray fucking sweats.

His abdominal muscles were more defined than I had ever seen. I followed them down and jerked my eyes back up when they found something I wasn't meant to see.

Shaking my head, I ran to him and patted his bare chest with both hands, grinning so hard my cheeks hurt. "I have a date."

"I heard," he said, smirking. "What is Benny's?"

Under normal circumstances, I would've scolded him for eavesdropping, but I couldn't bring myself to care. Nothing could spoil my mood right now. "It's a bar, and they just happen to be throwing their annual costume party tonight."

He cocked a brow. "And what will you be going as?"

My smile fell as my brain caught up. "I don't know."

"He did say to wear something... What was it? 'Nice?'" Jack laughed as he pushed off the door frame. He strolled to the counter and lifted a muffin, pulling the paper off before taking a bite. "Damn, this is good."

"Thanks," I said, suddenly distracted again. "I need to find a costume. What does 'nice' mean?"

Jack grinned as his gaze lifted back to mine. When he set the muffin down and closed the distance between us, I stood straighter, my cheeks flushing for some unknown reason. "I think you know what it means."

"Hot?" I asked, tilting my face to his. *Why is he so close? Why is he so tall?*

He cocked his head to the side, a smirk curving his lips as he tucked a strand of my hair behind my ear. "Scalding."

"Come with me to the costume shop?" The words fell from my lips before I had a chance to consider them, but I didn't regret asking, not as excitement sparked in his eyes.

"I would love nothing more."

My stomach flipped. Somehow, I knew he meant that.

I took a step back, resuming space between us. I needed air to breathe that didn't smell like Jack and cloud my mind the way he did—definitely an airborne disease.

"All right. Let me go change." I gestured down to my flour-covered tank top and pajama shorts, my fuzzy socks the only things left unscathed. How a baker who'd been baking for literal decades could still be such a mess, I had no clue.

As I turned for the door, I mindlessly added, "I don't think a dirty, scantily clad baker was what he had in mind when he said nice."

Jack groaned behind me, and I forced myself to not look back.

"Then, he's a fool," he muttered under his breath.

Thank the Ghouls, I didn't turn around because my mouth was hanging wide open. I snapped it shut and hurried out of the kitchen to my room.

JACK HELD the umbrella over both of us while I carried our two coffees.

The air was crisp, and the temperature dropped with each passing hour. Tonight would be *cold* at this rate.

As we stepped under the overhang, he closed the umbrella and held the door open for me. "Lead the way, little monster."

I rolled my eyes but stepped inside, shivering at the sudden warmth. Nerves had bundled and settled in my stomach as the day passed and we inched closer to tonight. It would be Eddy and I's first date, maybe my first kiss.

Excitement wrenched my chest, and I sucked in a deep breath. "Okay, what were we thinking?"

"Hmm." He skimmed the aisle of costumes. "How *'hot'* are we thinking?"

"What about a nurse?" I asked, pointing to a white dress with a red cross and a stethoscope.

"We can do better than that." Grinning, he lifted a costume—if it could be called that. It was merely a few scraps of black fabric. "How about this?"

"Is that a stripper costume?" I definitely didn't have the confidence for that, but Ghouls, I wished I did as Jack held it up to my form, and his eyes darkened. I swatted his hand away. "Is it weird that we're doing this together?"

He chuckled and replaced the costume. "Why would it be weird?"

"Because you're..." I turned away from him as I said the next words, pretending to look over the costume makeup. "You, and I'm me, and we're looking at clothes when the goal is to be *hot*."

"I think looking hot is in my wheel of expertise, don't you?"

I whipped around to him, and he was much closer than I anticipated. My lips parted on a gasp, and his eyes flitted to my mouth before he held up another costume.

"A police officer?" I arched a brow and placed a hand on his chest, pushing him away.

He didn't budge. Instead, he stepped *closer.*

"Would you rather be the prisoner?" he asked. I inched back, and he leaned forward. My ass hit the shelf, knocking over a few bottles of glitter hair spray, as his hands braced on either side of me. "You do seem like you may have an affinity for handcuffs."

The room was suddenly warm, and heat rose under my skin.

"What?" My face jerked back as I sputtered, "I do not —Why—"

His mouth ticked up as he lifted his hand to reveal a pair of furry handcuffs. "These don't speak to you?"

Yes. I blinked rapidly and shook my head.

He clicked his tongue and took a step back as he replaced them on the hook. "Lying is not a good look for you, little monster."

"I'm not lying," I spat as I followed after him.

His gaze roamed over the shelves while mine roamed

over the worn black T-shirt clinging to his torso. Lean muscles pulled the fabric taut over his form, tapering to a V that led to his black jeans...

I grabbed his arm and swiveled him toward me to stop my gaze from devouring his backside. "I'm not lying."

"Yes, you are," he said with a sureness he couldn't possibly feel. "But it's all right if you're not ready to admit that to me yet."

With that, he turned back to the shelves. *Yet?*

I was frozen on the spot. My mind briefly—*very* briefly—explored the possibility as he turned the corner and disappeared from sight. A flash of Jack in his gray sweats and what they so clearly outlined, coupled with a pair of handcuffs and his bed deepened the flush in my cheeks.

I shook my head and jogged after him.

This is not good. Not good at all.

As I turned the corner, my steps slowed. His eyes were glued to a tiny silk dress and a pair of fluffy white wings. Slowly, he turned to me with a devilish grin. Before I had a chance to reply, he lifted it off the rack.

"Yep," he hummed and strode toward the register. "This is the one."

12

DEVIL IN DISGUISE

I was hardly dressed for the weather, but damn, I looked good if I didn't say so myself.

It was so different than what I normally wore, but Jack was right about the angel costume. There was no way Eddy would be able to take his eyes off me.

Paired with my strappy gold heels, the silk dress left nothing to the imagination, only falling slightly below my ass. The thin straps wrapped over my shoulders and led to a deep V that revealed my lifted cleavage—basically a silk slip worn. The feathered wings were a bit difficult to get on, but they were surprisingly nice.

I'd let Eliza do my makeup. Well, she had insisted and squealed when I agreed. When I glanced in the mirror, I barely recognized myself. I tended to do my makeup dark, but she had done it light in every regard. My eyes were dusted with gold shimmer, my lips glossed with sheer pink. She also tinted my cheeks and nose with pink, the look somehow bringing out the freckles that already speckled across my nose.

"I look...sweet," I said before bursting into laughter.

I don't know why I laughed—perhaps it was the absurdity of a vampire disguised as an angel or the fact that I was about to go into public like this. A stiff wind would reveal my entire ass to the world as the only underwear I could manage was a tiny thong. Anything else would have shown through the thin white fabric.

"Like an angel," Eliza said, wiggling her brows.

She looped a dainty, dangling necklace around my neck. A long gold chain hung from it, reaching down between my breasts, tipped with a small teardrop diamond. The final touch—a halo—was attached to a headband that she slid over my messily curled hair.

"There," she said. "You look *good*. Eddy is going to hit his knees when he sees you."

Eliza, Robert, and I all took a shot of tequila together before I walked out, then ran back in for one more. Liquid courage, as they say.

When I neared the bar, I could hear the music before I saw the front. The music was loud, thumping through the air as the purple flickering lights lit the sidewalk.

My heart was in my throat as I stepped in line. When it was my turn, I showed the bouncer my ID and refrained from rolling my eyes; I was old enough to be his grandmother.

He grinned at me and waved me through. "Have a nice night, sweetheart."

"I'll try," I muttered, but when I stepped inside, my feet froze in place.

It was packed and loud. The music vibrated the floors as the scent of alcohol and perfume permeated the air, along with anticipation and excitement. Every person was dressed in a costume, some entirely hidden behind masks.

Smiling to myself, I weaved through the crowd toward

the bar. As I hopped on an empty bar stool, the bartender—a slashed murder victim—waved and did a double take. His eyes flashed to my exposed cleavage before dipping back to the bottle of alcohol in his hand. He quickly poured a drink and strolled over to me.

"Whatcha want?" he asked.

"What do you recommend?" I rested my chin on my palm.

He smiled and winked before opening the fridge to pull out a small plastic container. He sat it on the bar in front of me and said, "Candy corn jello shot."

My eyes widened. "That sounds good."

"Careful, they're strong."

I rolled my eyes and popped the lid off. Swiping my finger around the edge of the jello, I loosened it and tipped it back, chewing slowly as I held his gaze. "I'll be all right."

He crossed his arms over his chest and nodded. "Understood."

I started to hand him my debit card when he held up his hands and backed away. "On the house, angel."

"Thank you," I said, amused. "Wait. Can I have one more?"

"Sure thing." He laughed and handed me another.

The sweet jello slid down my throat when a hand landed on my shoulder, and I turned to find Eddy, dressed as a skeleton. My hand covered my mouth as I stifled my laugh. He'd shaved his beard to paint a skull on his face, but it looked like a child had painted it.

"Don't laugh," he said, even as he fought a laugh of his own. "I tried my best..." His words trailed off when his eyes slid down my body, taking in my costume, and his smile fell a fraction. "Although, your best seems to be much better than mine. You look—"

"Nice?" I shimmied my shoulders which caused the feather wings to sway and ruffle. His eyes followed this movement.

"Incredible," he breathed, then waved at the bartender. "Hey, buddy, can we get two spiked apple ciders down here?"

The bartender's gaze flicked to me, and he lifted a brow. I shrugged my shoulders, biting my lip so I wasn't grinning like an idiot. With that, he poured two mugs of cold apple cider and set them in front of us. Eddy handed him cash as I grabbed one mug and took a sip, suppressing a wince. It was nothing like Aggie's cider.

But Eddy was here, and I was his date.

Good Ghouls, I cannot believe this is actually happening.

As the warmth of alcohol started to spread through me, I relaxed a bit, and the music's bass thumped in my chest.

"Want to dance?" Eddy asked, following my line of sight to the swaying crowd.

"Sure," I replied casually, like I hadn't been waiting an entire decade for this moment.

I tipped back the rest of the cider; it burned its way down my throat and warmed my belly. My head was just the right amount of fuzzy—the kind that rid me of any insecurity. Tonight was going to be fun, and I was ready for it.

Eddy smiled and did the same before looping his hand in mine and tugging me onto the dance floor.

I DIDN'T SEE him at first, the devil in the corner watching me.

We'd been dancing for at least an hour, maybe two or three, only stopping to go back and forth to the bar when needed. A sheen of sweat had formed over my skin, my cheeks and legs burning from laughing and dancing to the erratic Halloween rave music. It was *glorious*.

But I knew. I felt his gaze on me after a few songs. I didn't acknowledge him, though. I let him watch, and it shot a thrill through me. His gaze was locked on my swaying body, even among the hundreds of women here.

I was horrible, depraved—dancing with the man I'd pined over for so long while another man watched me grind on him, but I didn't care. It set me aflame in a way I had never felt.

My devil sat with a drink in hand, reclined with one ankle thrown over his knee. His hair was black as night with two red horns protruding from the top of his head and his eyes bright red with contacts. His black button-up was unbuttoned down his chest, and his black slacks were pressed.

When he caught me looking, he smiled and revealed the dimple I knew would be there as he lifted his glass to me, dipping his chin.

He was magnificent—distracting, and I *let* him distract me. Perhaps it was the alcohol, or perhaps it was the warm, spicy scent that had taken root in my nose. He was the only thing I could smell, the only thing I could focus on. It was as if the crowd stayed parted the entire night, just so we had a clear view of each other.

His eyes never left me, and Eddy never even noticed.

13

THE DEVIL'S TEMPTATION

As Eddy walked away for a moment, I looked over my shoulder, and the devil lifted his hand, curling two fingers in a motion to come.

"Aren't you a sweet, little angel?" he purred when I neared him.

"Sometimes." I shrugged.

His mouth tilted up in a smirk as he extended a hand to me. I slid mine into it, and he pulled me forward. Slowly, I stepped one leg over his lap and then the other, straddling him. I started to glance over my shoulder, but he gripped my chin and turned my gaze back to his.

"Don't look for anyone but me while you're on my lap," he said, his tone commanding.

Something deep in my chest fluttered.

My eyes were glued to his, my lips parted, as his hand slid from my jaw to the back of my head. It knotted in my hair and ripped my head back. My eyes fell closed as his mouth skimmed along my jaw but not my lips.

But I *wanted* it. I wanted more.

"I don't think an angel should be this tempting," he whispered, his fingertips sliding down my spine.

"I'm not tempting," I whispered back, breathless.

His hand paused on my lower back. "You are the embodiment of temptation."

He pulled me closer until my chest was flush with his, and then I felt it—him hardening beneath me.

I should have come to my senses. I should have gotten up and left, or slapped him for doing this when I was on my first date with Eddy. But I did none of those things.

Instead, I ground my hips against him. He groaned into my neck and nipped at my skin, pulling a gasp from me. His hand snaked beneath the silk dress and gripped my ass. He let out a breathy laugh as he found my bare cheek; the only fabric separating me from his trousers was the tiny thong I'd nearly forgotten about.

I licked my lips, my breaths leaving me in pants as his mouth continued its exploration.

I don't know what possessed me to say this, but nothing could have stopped the words from tumbling from my mouth. "If you're the devil, then I want to sin just to be in hell with you."

He smiled into my neck and bit me again, harder. I arched into him, letting my head fall back, and to my complete surprise, my canines lengthened. I ran my tongue over the pointed tips as the sudden desire to bite him back surged in me. I wanted his blood to run down my chin while his cock—

"Good fucking girl. You'd be *exactly* where you belong, little monster."

Oh, Ghouls. My body was on fire. Something deep inside me was going to combust if I didn't get more: more friction, more him, something, anything.

"I need...I need..." I moaned as his hand slipped farther beneath the dress and up to my waist. Everyone around us would be able to see my ass if they looked hard enough, but again, I couldn't care less, and apparently, neither could he.

I was utterly and thoroughly burning.

"I know what you need," he whispered.

"Jack," I moaned when he ground his hardened length against my barely concealed, soaked core.

His face lifted from my neck, his gaze sliding past me. "Better go back to your little date, baby. He's looking for you."

I gasped, blinking rapidly. He pulled his hands from beneath my dress and tapped my hips, and I slid from his lap as a small wave of guilt washed over me. I bit my lip, swallowing hard as I glanced over my shoulder and backed away from him.

"Don't." Jack stood in front of me and gripped my chin to turn my face to him, his gaze heated, demanding. "Don't feel guilty over this. Not over me. You may not have accepted it yet, but you *are* mine."

His thumb ran over my bottom lip, and I was mesmerized. Even as I knew Eddy was nearby, looking for me, Jack had my complete attention.

"Have your fun. Dance, drink, kiss, fuck, I don't care. I'll be here waiting for you when you're ready." Holding my gaze, he downed the rest of his whiskey and set the glass on the table with a clink before striding into the crowd.

Tucked in the back pocket of his slacks was a pair of metal handcuffs.

My eyes were glued to the glint of silver as I stood there, mouth agape and cheeks burning, unable to process what just happened. I stared after him long after he was gone.

"Oh, there you are," Eddy said, his arm snaking around

my waist, and I bit back the sudden urge to step away from Eddy.

Jack's touch was burned into my skin and his words echoed through my mind. *You are mine.*

Shaking my head, I glanced up at Eddy and plastered a smile on my face.

His?

14

THE MONSTER FINALLY COMES

My head and body were still warm from the liquor as I waved goodbye to Eddy and walked in the front door of the Dead and Breakfast. I silently closed it behind me, as it was well after three a.m. and everyone would undoubtedly be asleep.

I strolled into my room and tugged the angel wings off.

Don't do it.

I'd been fighting myself the entire walk home, and now, as I glanced in the mirror, watching myself pull the halo off, I knew it was for naught. I tossed it on the dresser and yanked my heels off.

Leaving nothing but the silk dress, I took a shaky breath and padded into the hallway.

Turn around.

I smirked.

No.

I walked up the stairs and down the hallway, all the way to the end. Standing before his door, I took a deep breath and quietly turned the door knob. The door swung open slowly, and I peeked into his room.

It was dark, too dark to make anything out. My breaths and hands shook, but I stepped in and closed the door behind me, reclining on it, letting my head fall back on the wood. Jack's scent filled this room more than any other; it was delicious, and I needed a moment to bask in it.

Pushing off the door, I took a cautious step toward the bed, inching closer in an attempt to make out his form.

"Hi, baby."

I froze. He stood directly behind me, close enough that I could feel his breath on my neck. My breath hitched, my stomach flipping.

His hand snaked beneath the silk dress and slid up to my waist. He groaned as his hand splayed over my abdomen just beneath my breasts, and his other hand found my throat and pulled me flush to his chest.

"Couldn't resist?" he whispered.

"Couldn't sleep," I replied, breathless.

His chest shook with a chuckle, warm as he pressed into my back. His hand slid higher, his thumb grazing the underside of my breast, pulling a gasp from me. "What's on your mind?"

I paused. I knew he could feel my erratic breaths beneath his fingertips. My throat bobbed, and I whispered, *"Everything."*

He groaned, biting the connection of my neck and shoulder. His teeth dug in hard enough to bruise, and my head fell back onto his chest as my own canines lengthened for the second time. It reignited the burn in my core with a vengeance. *Ghouls, this is depraved.*

"You can have everything, baby. You'll take all of me and do it beautifully."

His hand rose higher to cup my breast. No one had ever

touched me here, and when he pinched my nipple, sparks flashed behind my lids.

"I just...I just want to learn." My hands found him behind me, gripping his bare thighs, and I realized he was wearing nothing but boxer briefs. I groaned internally. "I've never..."

He smiled against my skin and tightened his grip around my throat. "You've never been touched here?" He moved to the other breast and flicked his finger across my nipple. I moaned, shaking my head. "Then you've definitely never been touched where I just *know* you're burning up, have you?"

I shook my head again.

"Are you aching for me, baby?" He ground his hips into my ass, and I arched.

"Yes." The word left me on a pant.

"I would love nothing more than to teach you, little monster, but tell me... When I teach you how to fuck and you take this sweet, little pussy back to Eddy, are you going to be thinking of me while you ride him?"

I choked, my breath leaving me in a whoosh as my cheeks flushed. Before I could say a word, his hand tightened and cut off my air. I dug my nails into his thigh, and he groaned into my neck, grinding his hips harder into me as if my nails were a tease, as if he *wanted* it.

He walked me forward until my thighs were pressed against the side of the bed and only then did he loosen his grip around my throat. I inhaled sharply, swiveling on my heel toward him. His hand cupped my jaw and tilted my face to his, a vicious smirk on his lips that cleared every thought from my head.

I jumped as his hand found my hip, and he chuckled,

letting his finger trail up over my waist and between my breasts. Chills erupted in his wake.

"Are you sure you want this?"

I swallowed hard and nodded.

"No, baby, I need to hear you say the words."

My cheeks flamed, and I was overwhelmingly grateful for the darkness. "Y-Yes."

His finger slid along my collarbone to the strap of my small dress. His other slid into my hair, and I let my head fall back into his grasp as he slid the strap of my dress off my shoulder. It fell down my arm, exposing one breast.

He didn't waste a second.

I gasped as he took my nipple in his mouth—warm and sucking. My body bowed into him, and he groaned around me.

His hand slid from my hair to push the other sleeve off my shoulder. With that, the dress fell to the floor, leaving nothing but my thong.

And then, like the worst possible thing I could think of, he let me go.

A whimper left me as my eyes shot open, but it was too dark to see anything other than his silhouette as he took two large steps back.

"Jack?"

A lamp clicked on. Dim, warm light washed over the room.

Biting my lip, I blinked rapidly as my mind warred between covering myself or holding my chin high, but I didn't have time to decide as he strolled back to me. His gaze slowly poured over my form, taking in every single inch.

As his eyes devoured me, mine dipped to his bulging

boxers. The blush in my cheeks deepened, burning worse than it ever had.

His hands found me again, sliding down my waist as he sank to his knees in front of me. "Perhaps you are an angel."

With a mind of their own, my fingers slid into his hair, and he flashed me a devastating grin.

"Why is that?" My voice sounded much too breathless, too needy, but I didn't care. Not right now.

"Because nothing else could possibly be *this* fucking beautiful."

His tongue flicked out and circled around my nipple, pulling a moan from my lips, as his hands slid lower, lower, lower—pulling my thong with them.

And then I was bare. Entirely bare.

This was the first time I'd ever been naked in front of a man, and I felt much more confident than I imagined I would. Perhaps it was the alcohol or the dim lighting, but I felt...warm. Hot. Burning.

There was no room for insecurity among the desperate sureness that filled me. I was comfortable with Jack—for some unfathomable reason I was not going to explore right now—and I wanted this. I wanted to be touched and fucked and Ghouls, I wanted to be kissed like a woman should be.

But that damned clause I insisted on prevented it.

Adrenaline shot through my veins when Jack lifted me by my waist and set me on the bed.

"I'm a virgin." The words escaped before I could stop them, and I snapped my mouth shut, closing my eyes.

His chuckle pulled them open again. "I know, little monster. I'll go slow..." He held my gaze as he dipped his head lower, my breath hitching as he pressed a kiss to the inside of my thigh. "Until you ask me otherwise."

Would I ask him for that? Will I even be able to form words at all? He dropped his eyes and pulled my legs apart slowly. His smile deepened, revealing his dimple. *I doubt it.*

As his lips edged closer and closer to the apex of my thighs, my breathing quickened, but I couldn't pull my eyes away. When his mouth found my core—namely his tongue—my head fell back.

"Oh, my Ghouls," I breathed.

His hand grazed over my skin to my jaw and jerked my face back to him. His blue eyes were icy, nearly glowing with heat. "It's not the Ghouls tasting you right now, baby."

With his gaze on me, he dipped his face back down to run his tongue along me, and I bit back a moan.

He clicked his tongue. "Don't silence those pretty little sounds. I want to hear them *all.*"

I... There were no words in my brain. As he dove back in, he released my chin, and my head fell back again, my eyes falling closed. He was merciless, eating me like a starved man, and I was... *What am I?*

He nipped at my clit, and a loud gasp escaped me. He sucked away the pain before swirling his tongue with a groan.

Delirious. I'm delirious.

A ball of sparks curled in my lower belly as he increased his pace. My breaths left me quicker, my pants and moans matching their pace. One of his hands found my waist, gripping me tight enough to bruise, while the other slid between my breasts. He paused his mouth long enough to gently push me back onto the bed.

As soon as I was horizontal, he gripped my waist and yanked me down until my ass was nearly hanging off the bed. He lifted my legs above his shoulders and slid his tongue *into* me as his thumb circled over my sensitive clit.

"Jack," I moaned, bowing from the bed. My hands wound into his hair. "Please, I need... I need..."

"Come for me, baby," he whispered, the words caressing me nearly as much as his tongue.

I shattered, a sound halfway between a scream and a moan filling my ears as sparks blinded my vision. My hands fisted his hair, my back bowing off the bed entirely. Wave after wave of ecstasy rolled through me as his tongue continued, dragging out the orgasm as long as possible until it was nearly painful.

I didn't immediately fall from the high; rather, I floated along the euphoric clouds, my eyes still closed, as he slid from beneath my limp legs and crawled up my body. When his hand slid the hair back from my face, I cracked an eye open at him to find him grinning like a madman, his lips shining with my desire.

I laughed and swatted at his shoulder. "Stop looking at me like that."

"Like what?" He cocked a brow and licked his lips. "Like a person who's just tasted a new drug for the first time?" My smile fell a fraction. "One that is overwhelmingly addictive." He kissed my jaw, my neck, my collarbone. "And delicious and—"

I knotted my hands in his hair and jerked his face back up to mine. His eyes widened as if he hadn't expected it but quickly resumed their normal warmth.

We froze, the air electrified between us.

A beat passed. I inhaled slowly, sliding my hand from his hair, and he tilted his head to the side, a curiously soft smile on his lips.

"Do you still want to continue? We can—"

"Yes." While nerves curled in my stomach, the need for *more* overwhelmed every other feeling.

I reached between us, down to his boxer briefs, and ran a hand along his hardened length, swallowing hard at his size. Satisfaction swelled in my chest as he groaned and rocked his hips into my hand.

Hooking my fingers in the waistband, I slowly pulled them down, and he never broke eye contact. When they got low enough, he kicked them off but kept space between us. I wound my arms around his waist to pull him down to me, gasping when his length pressed into my thigh. His bare skin was warm against mine.

"It may hurt at first," he said. My chest tightened but quickly relaxed when he kissed along my jaw, my neck, my shoulder, and back up, leisurely exploring my body. "But it won't for long, I promise."

My shaky inhale was audible as he slid his hand down my waist to my hip. Slowly, he reached between my thighs and pulled them apart, spreading me wide so he could settle between them. The tip of his length pressed against my core, and my hips bucked.

"Easy, baby. We move at your pace," he murmured, and I nodded, meeting his gaze. He rested his palm on my cheek. "Ready?"

The truest word I'd ever spoken slipped past my lips, "Yes."

He eased into me, then, just the tip, and I gasped at the invasion, my back arching as my body tensed.

"Hey," he whispered. "Keep your eyes on me, baby. I want to *see* you as you feel my cock for the first time."

I whimpered at his words, but he nodded in approval when I met his gaze again. Ever so slowly, he moved again, inching further inside me, and I fought the urge to stop him. My nails dug into his shoulders, filling the air around us with the warm scent of his blood.

I didn't want him to stop, but the pressure building in my core was nearly unbearable

How much more of him could there be?

"Quick pinch, okay?"

I nodded, and he thrust his hips in one quick motion. I scrunched my eyes as pain laced through me, but he pulled out and reentered slowly. The pain dissipated bit by bit, inch by inch as he filled me, chasing the pain away with a deliciously new fullness.

He slid a finger down between us and swiped his finger along his length. When he lifted it again, it was tinged red, a small bit of blood on his fingertip—*my* blood.

I parted my lips, watching him intently, but it was when he slid the finger into his mouth and sucked that I lost it. My canines extended, and I couldn't pull my eyes away from his mouth.

"Delicious," he whispered, sliding his length back in.

I moaned, my brows furrowing and body tensing as he filled me to his entirety and paused. This was...

I had no words. No words at all.

Just this stunningly intense feeling.

"Still with me?" He pulled out to the tip, and I nearly felt empty at his absence. As he slid back in, my mouth fell open on another moan, and his smirk returned to reveal the dimple in his cheek.

I wound my hand in his black hair and grinned as I swirled my hips. "Still here."

He groaned and pulled out before slamming back in, tearing a scream from my throat.

"God, I don't think I've heard anything more beautiful." His eyes darkened. It seemed the room itself darkened around us. "I need to hear it again and again and *again*."

With that, he slid his hands under my ass, lifted my

hips, and held me to him. I didn't have a second to process anything before he thrust into me hard enough to make my eyes roll back. He thrust again and again, just like he promised, and I knew the sounds filling the room were mine, echoing in his ears like a cheer, a praise.

My head swam with ecstasy, a sheen of sweat covering my skin as I wrapped my arms around his neck and melted into him. His pace was intoxicating—fast and hard, satisfying every deep need I hadn't realized plagued me until now as he obliterated each and every one.

"Fuck, Jack. Fuck, fuck, fuck," I mumbled until my words became incoherent.

He smiled against my skin, his breathing fanning across my cheek. "Yes, baby. Tell me how good it feels."

"So…" My grip tightened around his neck. He slid a hand from beneath me to circle a thumb over my clit, and the next words tore from me. "Good. So fucking *good*."

And even that was an understatement.

He felt euphoric.

While he satisfied every deep, desperate, aching need for now, I *knew* he was also creating new ones. Stronger, more demanding ones. I could feel it with each powerful stroke as he touched my fucking soul, marking me with a new desire.

He was so right—a new, addictive, delicious drug.

He pounded into me as his thumb swirled over my clit. I could do nothing but hold on and hope I didn't explode as I built and built. There was too much sensation: his cock, his thumb, his body pressed into mine, his damned scent filling my lungs. The only part of me free of him was my mouth, and I didn't *want* it to be free of him.

"Jack." My fingernails dug into his skin, and the rich scent of his blood surrounded me.

"Come for me again, little monster." His tongue flicked out and touched my pointed canines. I sucked in a breath but didn't bite. "Let me feel you fall apart around my cock."

He increased his pace with both his cock and his thumb, and I rocked my hips, matching his rhythm. His mouth found my breast again, sucking and swirling his tongue over my nipple, and it was too much.

Not two thrusts later, I was lost. I clenched around him, vaguely hearing his name spill from my lips on a loud moan. My vision blacked as my eyes rolled back, and he groaned, coming at the same time, filling me.

When I came down this time, it felt like I had fallen from the heavens. My body was limp and useless, my eyes still closed and my arms hanging loosely around his neck, but Ghouls, I was fucking satisfied in a way I had never known.

He slid my hair back, his cock still twitching inside me. "Such a perfect little monster."

15

BREAKFAST AT REMI'S

The early morning daylight peeked through my window.

Groaning, I threw the covers back and sat up, stretching my arms up, cracking a few joints before I hopped out of bed. I didn't feel any different—other than a deep satisfaction and a delicious soreness between my legs.

In a shocking turn of events, I didn't feel guilty like I thought I might. Instead, I felt...good. I just hoped Jack wouldn't act differently. It was a hook-up, and he knew that. My first time, but a one-night stand all the same.

After giving myself a once over in the mirror, I walked to the kitchen, yawning as I strolled around the corner, then stopped in my tracks. Jack sat in a kitchen chair with his feet propped up on the table, sipping from a cup of coffee.

"Good morning, little monster." His tone was casual, but I still narrowed my eyes at him as I made my way to the sink and quickly washed my hands.

Grabbing the towel, I reclined on the counter and studied his smug face as I dried my hands. "Are you going to be...different now?"

"Different?" He grinned, cocking a dark brow. His blue eyes seemed brighter today. "Why would I be different?"

My mouth opened and snapped shut. I turned to pull out breakfast supplies, setting the metal bowl on the counter along with the flour and sugar. "Oh, no reason."

I startled when he stepped up behind me, sliding one hand over my waist while the other set a mug of steaming coffee on the counter—my mug, an orange pumpkin cup that I used every morning.

"Hmm, let's see. Why would I be different?" His hand roamed over my body, tracing every curve as he drew out his words, setting me on edge. "Because you came on my dick? Or because you did so while crying out my name to the heavens like a prayer?"

My cheeks burned, my eyes wide as I froze with my hand in the utensil drawer. A second passed, and I swiveled back to him, pointing the wooden spoon at him. "This changes nothing. You know who I'm after, who...who I want."

His smile deepened. He nodded, holding his hands up. "Just sex, then. Got it."

"You think we're going to do that again?" My brows furrowed, my head cocked to the side.

He chuckled as he brought his mug to his lips. "You don't?"

I hadn't considered doing it again. I didn't respond; instead, I turned back to the counter, biting my lips against the smile threatening to reveal my thoughts.

"Honestly, it'll probably help the whole fake dating ruse."

I rolled my eyes. "Oh, yeah, sure. *That's* why you want to do me again."

"Oh, no." He slid his finger beneath the strap of my tank

top. It moved higher over my shoulder and down my chest where his fingers skimmed over my breast. "I want to '*do you*' again because you're addictive."

My breathing stopped as he leaned down to my ear.

"I fear you may be the darkness that calls to me and my magic, sweet, little monster. If I stayed long enough, you would undoubtedly be my undoing."

I blinked rapidly, swallowing hard. *Why does that sound so good? That's ridiculous.*

"It doesn't work like that." I gritted my teeth when my words sounded as breathless as I felt.

"Doesn't it?" His breath tickled my ear as he whispered, "Don't worry. I'll be your dirty little secret for the rest of the month, then I'll leave, and you can pretend this never happened."

I scoffed. *Yeah, like I could ever forget his—*

He slid his hand under my chin and turned my face toward his, grinning as he dipped his face down to mine. My chest clenched, but I froze. At the last second, he shifted to the left and slid his lips along my cheek. I closed my eyes, swallowing hard before he pulled back and swiped a thumb over my bottom lip.

"How often do you have to drink blood?"

The question caught me off guard, and my head flinched back an inch. "About once a month, really. It's not as often as you would think."

"Have you had any since my arrival two and a half weeks ago?"

"No. Why?"

He reached into the drawer and pulled out a knife. My chest clenched, my gaze locked on the blade. *Surely, he's not—*

He pushed the point of the blade into his fingertip and peeked up at me. "Well? Where do you want it?"

Shocked, I slowly pushed my coffee cup along the counter, so it was beneath his hand. I swallowed hard as the drop of blood rolled down his finger, my head tilting to the side to follow it. He grinned and held it over the black coffee, letting more than a few drops fall into the dark liquid.

"Is that enough?" he asked.

I nodded, my heart oddly warm. "You're concerned about me?"

"Is concern the right word?" He pushed the cup back and lifted a hand to the back of his neck, running it up and down. "I just noticed, and well...I have blood, and you drink blood. Seemed like the friendly thing to do."

Is he embarrassed? I stifled a smile and lifted it to my lips. As I took a large gulp, my eyes closed, my head falling back as an involuntary moan escaped me. His blood was as warm and spicy as his scent; it *was* his scent. That intoxicating smell that had been torturing me all this time, calling to me, it was his blood, and it tasted...

"Delicious," I breathed. When I opened my eyes again, I found him watching me intently, his gaze heated and locked on my lips.

His throat bobbed. "All right. I'm going to go take a cold shower. I'll be back for breakfast." He walked toward the doorway and paused, looking over his shoulder to let his eyes dip down my body. "God, I love your pajamas."

I inhaled slowly as he disappeared down the hall and took another long drink of the blood-infused coffee—my favorite way to take it.

How has my life changed so drastically in a couple of weeks?

I made breakfast and placed it out in a daze, merely going through the motions as thoughts of Jack's mouth between my thighs took the forefront of my mind.

It wasn't until everyone started filing in for breakfast that I blinked and cleared my throat. When Jack entered again, his smile was smug. He was wearing those damned sweatpants again, and I fought valiantly to not let my eyes lower, I swear I did.

He winked at me from across the room when he caught me staring, and I jerked my gaze away, which coincidentally landed on Eddy.

My thoughts froze before racing at a million miles an hour, my chest constricting. He smiled sheepishly as he strolled over to me and leaned on the counter beside me.

"Mind if I join you for breakfast?" he asked, tilting his head to the side.

I smiled, my eyes flicking to the kitchen table and back to him. "Of course."

With a deep breath, I grabbed the last pot of coffee and mug tree to bring to the table, locking eyes with Jack as I set them down. His grin was small, daring, as he lifted a brow and patted the empty seat next to him. I exhaled slowly and took the seat beside Jack as Eddy sat on the other side of me, leaving me conveniently sandwiched between the two.

Oh, good Ghouls.

"Good morning, guys," Eddy said.

Jack turned toward him, resting his chin on his fist with amusement. "Morning, Ed."

Eddy stared, his mouth forced up in a tight smile. "Jack."

With that, breakfast started as normal, and I released a breath of relief—until Jack opened his mouth again.

"Remi, remind me to tell Aggie thank you for booking me a room here with you." He refilled his coffee mug and took a sip. "Your place really is so nice. I've enjoyed my stay *immensely*."

I sputtered on my coffee. Eddy stared daggers at Jack, a muscle ticking in his jaw.

"Isn't it? We love staying here," Eliza said, oblivious as she placed one of each pastry on her plate. "Remi always makes sure everything is so comfy, cozy."

Robert laughed awkwardly, his eyes darting between the two men as he patted his wife's hand.

"Oh, yes." Jack's eyes flashed, and I closed mine for a second, pressing my lips into a tight line. "*So* cozy."

"Seems like I need to book a room sometime," Eddy said.

My stomach flipped. "Sure. Anytime."

"You know, most people say three's a crowd." Jack leaned in closer to my ear with his eyes on Eddy as he whispered only loud enough for us to hear, "I say three's a party."

I gasped and choked, coughing into my hand. Eddy's face jerked back slightly, his lip curling back to reveal his white teeth. He clenched his jaw and turned his face away.

"Not into that?" Jack shrugged his shoulders. "Just thought I'd throw it out there."

Wait.

My gaze slowly shifted to Jack, and he winked at me over his mug.

No, wait. I think... Am I into that?

IRRITATION HAD BUBBLED in my chest the more I thought about Jack's comments at breakfast, but when I jogged up to his side as he headed into town, it overflowed into a boiling pot of anger.

"Do you enjoy torturing me?"

He glanced over his shoulder and ran a hand through his black hair. "Of course I do."

I was prepared to argue, but his words choked off my own. My feet paused for a moment before I shook my head and continued walking beside him. "Why?"

He stopped and looked at me as if the answer was obvious.

"I like seeing you flustered, seeing you *squirm*." His grin was devilish, as it often was. I was beginning to wonder if he *was* the devil, if his costume at the party was merely confirmation. Perhaps he'd already shown me who he truly was. "It's quickly becoming my favorite pastime."

My mouth hung open, my eyes narrowing. "What is wrong with you?"

The smile slid from his face, his head tilting to the side as he stepped into me, his piercing eyes boring holes in my soul. "I told you the darkness called to me, little monster. That should've told you all you needed to know."

He ran a thumb over my burning cheeks, clicking his tongue. I should've walked away, but I was enraptured by the way his eyes devoured me, even as it nearly made me want to crawl out of my skin. My feet remained firmly planted where they were, but I crossed my arms over my chest, my jaw tight.

His mouth ticked up as he lowered to whisper, "You've got to start being more perceptive."

I rolled my eyes and jerked my face from his grasp. "Right. Got it," I said, striding down the sidewalk.

"See you tonight, Remi," he called out behind me.

Ah, the haunted house. I'd nearly forgotten, and I certainly hadn't talked to Jack about it. Nor would I be.

I waved over my shoulder at him without another word, and his laughter followed me as I made a beeline toward the dog shelter.

16

ACTUALLY, THE GREEN-EYED MONSTER IS A SLASHER

"I'm glad you asked me to come with you." Eddy threw an arm around my shoulders. "Friday Haunts are my favorite."

For the entirety of our friendship, him doing something like this would have set off a cacophony of butterflies in my stomach but not anymore, it seemed.

I'm getting more comfortable with him. I stifled a smile and snaked my arm around his waist—something I would've never done just a few weeks ago.

"I know you're seeing Jack, too." He gave me a quick squeeze and slid a finger under my chin to tip my head back. "But I hope you choose me in the end."

Screams erupted behind us. We jumped and swiveled around to find an actor who had scared the group behind us in line. The actor was tall, hidden behind black robes and a Ghostface mask.

Eddy squeezed me tighter to his side as the scare actor turned his sights on us, and a giggle bubbled in my throat. He stared behind his covered black eyes and shook his head, clicking his tongue before walking off in the other direction.

As the breeze blew, I inhaled deeply. Jack was nearby. The scent of his blood had amplified since I'd tasted it—a constant tease. I looked around, attempting to be nonchalant, but didn't see him.

Good.

When we made it to the front door, Eddy handed the doorman our tickets. The sound of screams and Halloween music drifted from the doorway along with the smoky, white haze creeping along the floor.

I took a deep, shaky breath as nerves bit at me and tightened my grip around Eddy's hand.

He glanced down at me, grinning. "It'll be all right."

I chuckled nervously and nodded as we stepped over the threshold.

The Haunted House was long and thorough, each room a different theme. We made it through the circus and the claustrophobia rooms with ease, but when we got to the pitch-black room, my chest clenched.

It was so dark, I could no longer see Eddy. A strobe light flashed, revealing exactly how small the room was and the only person inside it: a Ghostface with a knife. I screamed, releasing Eddy's hand as I stumbled backward.

Another flash of light, and I saw an actor lunge at Eddy. My breath hitched.

In the next flash, Eddy darted from the room.

A hand wrapped around my wrist, and I jerked against it. "You can't—What are you—"

Where is the damn light? It hadn't flashed again, and the room was darker than midnight. My head swam, adrenaline pouring through my veins, my limbs tingling.

I'm going to pass out.

The actor tugged my wrist and swiveled me around so that my arm was behind my back. A cry broke from my lips, and he walked me forward until my cheek was pressed into the cool wall. My breath left me in shaky waves until the actor leaned down to my neck, and my breathing stopped altogether.

The strobe light flashed again, a blinding purple.

He kissed the hollow of my throat, and I inhaled sharply —the warm, spicy scent invading my lungs like poison. My core started burning as if on command, and I gritted my teeth but stopped struggling. My throat bobbed.

Another flash.

Struggle, you idiot. Kick. Scream. Fight. Do something.

"Did you wear this slutty little dress for me?" He slid his fingers along the back of my thigh and slipped beneath the fabric of my black dress. I arched as his fingers grazed over my upper thigh—dangerously close to the desperate burn that had erupted.

"No. I wore it for Eddy."

Another flash, and he chuckled against my throat. "Sure you did, little monster."

Ghouls, get away from him. What are you doing?

He released my wrist and dropped to his knees behind me, his hands roaming down my body. Flutters woke in my lower belly as he widened my stance, jerked my hips back, and then...

Then, my cheeks flamed as he bit the tights that shielded my core and ripped a hole in them with his teeth.

When did he take that damned mask off?

The purple light flashed again, just long enough for me to see Jack's vicious smirk. I gasped and attempted to snap my legs together, but his knees prevented me as he crouched between them. He clicked his tongue again—that damned tongue.

The next flash of light illuminated his gaze, so heated I

was sure I would burst into flames if he kept looking at me like that.

"You're not wearing underwear." It wasn't a question.

I closed my eyes and pressed my face into the wall as embarrassment burned through me. I was just standing here, letting his eyes devour my core, knowing he would see how slick I already was.

My body responded to him that way. I couldn't help it.

Move. Move. Move.

His tongue slid along my clit, and I moaned, planting my hands on the wall.

Horrible. I'm so horrible.

"For someone who claims she doesn't want me, your pussy sure does tell another story," he whispered.

I bit my cheek, refusing to respond.

Another flash of light and his tongue found me again, swirling and flicking at a merciless pace. When two of his fingers slid into me, I screamed, not bothering to stifle it. It didn't matter as the group in the room next to us screamed, too, drowning out my own.

"Good girl," he hummed, and satisfaction rolled through me at his praise.

The purple strobe flashed again, and I got a glimpse of his face between my thighs. I whimpered when it disappeared because the sight of him was delicious; it curled the ball in my lower belly tighter, and I *loved* it.

As he pulled his fingers out and thrust three back in, moving fast—too fast for my body to catch up—my head fell back.

Another flash of light, and I was a wanton mess. My back arched to give him more access, my hips moving with his movement, reaching for more, my screams and moans lost to the haunted sounds all around us. I wanted more. I would have done just about anything for more in this moment.

Ghouls, I wanted *him*.

What the fuck is wrong with me?

As he hit the sensitive spot inside me relentlessly, I was nearly sobbing. His tongue, his fingers, his scent... My canines lengthened. The only thing that would make this more euphoric would be his blood on my tongue.

"Come for me, baby." The light flashed again, and he met my gaze. "Unless you want the next group to hear your screams, too."

I gasped as he nipped at my clit and sucked the pain away. One more flick of his tongue, and I was lost. A blinding orgasm ripped through me as my nails dug into the wall.

When he stood and turned me slowly, reality came crashing back and shockingly, I didn't care. Not one bit. Not right now.

The depravity set me aflame.

Jack, he... My eyes lifted, but I still couldn't see him. I felt him, though, his breath on my cheek, his chest pressed into mine. He would feel mine, too. We paused, breathing heavily. Somehow, the stark darkness almost felt comforting, like it offered the privacy I needed to allow myself to take whatever—*who*ever I wanted without shame, as if the daylight tomorrow wouldn't know what happened in the dark.

It freed me. *He* freed me.

But the light flashed again, and he was close—so very close. His hand quickly found my chin, and I gasped, my lips parting. He took the opportunity to slide his fingers into my mouth, and I whimpered around them.

When I closed my mouth and sucked, he groaned in

approval. "Taste how good you are," he whispered. "So fucking good."

My hands wound into his hair, and he popped his fingers from my mouth to slide his hands under my ass. He lifted me and slammed my back into the wall. He kissed my neck, my jaw, everything but my mouth, and I was breathless—lost.

With my canines extended, I kissed his throat, moving lower to where it met with his shoulder. He continued his perusal as I moved his shirt collar and licked his skin. He shuttered, and I smiled into him, grinding my hips against his hardened length.

Then I bit.

The light flashed, revealing the tensed muscles of his shoulder. I ran my fingertips up his spine to the back of his neck and knotted my hand in his hair as I sucked, the blood trickling from the small puncture wounds. We moaned simultaneously as his body crushed me against the wall, his fingers tightening around my ass hard enough to bruise.

The door opened, and a drunken group stumbled in, laughing.

Jack sighed into my neck. "Another time, little monster."

He set me on my feet, pulled his mask back down, and grabbed the knife from the back of his jeans.

The strobe light flashed as he turned toward them. Screams erupted, and I dashed from the room amidst the chaos, wiping my delirious smile with the back of my sleeve.

I made it through the rest of the house in a daze before I found Eddy standing outside, his brows furrowed and eyes glued to the exit. Relief flooded him as he strode toward me.

I narrowed my eyes at him, stifling a smile. "You left me in there!"

His eyes widened. "I am *so* sorry. They wouldn't let me go back and find you."

A giggle broke free as I shoved his shoulder, and he chuckled, grabbing my wrist and pulling me into him. He hugged me with his arms wrapped around my waist, his chest shaking with laughter.

An actor stepped from the side door, accompanied by Jack's scent, and I stood straighter, inhaling slowly.

I felt his gaze on me before I turned to confirm, and sure enough, reclining on the back wall of the building with his arms crossed over his chest was Jack, still hidden behind his costume.

Turning to Eddy, my chest clenched as I rested my palms on his cheeks. His smile lifted, his eyes dropping to my mouth, and without hesitation, I smiled and arched into him as I pulled his face down to mine. I kissed him slowly at first, but his hands tightened around my waist as he deepened it, the scruff along his chin tickling my skin. I groaned into his mouth, and he *growled*.

I pulled back an inch, my mouth falling open, eyes wide. "Did you...Did you just growl at me?"

His amber eyes flashed, and he wrapped a hand around the back of my head, pulling me back. His mouth crashed to mine and pulled a moan from my lips as he devoured me—right in front of Jack.

A sick wave of satisfaction rolled through me.

I WAVED bye to Eddy and barely made it two steps into the Dead and Breakfast when a hand wrapped around my throat, not tight enough to choke but enough to lead me. My hands grabbed his wrist, my jaw clenched.

I locked eyes with Jack as he backed me into my room, the corded muscles of his forearm revealed by his rolled-back sleeve.

"Did you think that was funny, little monster?" he whispered as he kicked the door shut behind us.

I smirked. "It was a little funny."

His grip tightened. I didn't have time to react as he pulled me forward, stopping with his lips an inch from mine. One tiny movement and we'd be breaking our deal, inking these marks into our skin for everyone to see, permanently.

But Ghouls, it almost felt worth it.

I swallowed hard, and he grinned, but it wasn't happy.

It was...wicked.

"Do you think it's funny that I can kiss every inch of you except where I *really* want to?" His breath tickled my skin, and he edged closer. My breath hitched. I attempted to pull back, but his hold was solid. "Do you think it was funny for me to have to watch you give your first kiss to someone so insignificant?"

My brows furrowed as my skin burned. *How did he know that was my first kiss?*

"He is not insignificant," I bit out against his choking grasp.

He shook his head, releasing a breathy laugh. "He will be."

What—

His lips nearly skimmed mine. My entire body tensed, frozen.

"Would it be so bad to have my mark on you forever? I kind of like the thought..." His blue eyes flared, locked on my mouth. "I *love* the thought."

"Jack," I whispered as panic flared.

"I told you to kiss and fuck whoever you want, but the next time you do it solely to get a rise from me, I *will* mark this into your skin. Permanently." I rolled my eyes, and his grip tightened around my throat. "And stop rolling your eyes at me, little monster."

With that, he released me and left, silently closing the door behind him.

What just happened? I smiled, biting my lip, my eyes wide as they fell to the floor. *Exactly what I wanted, it seems.*

I7

FUCK THE FEAR

A knock sounded on my bedroom door.

Squinting at the window, I groaned. Today was Sunday, my only day to sleep in, and someone was knocking at the crack of dawn.

Another aggravating knock and I threw the covers back to hop out of bed. I staggered to the door, shuffling my tired feet, and opened it to find Jack, dressed in all leather with a black helmet in hand.

He chuckled and leaned on the door frame. "You look...sleepy."

I glared at him. "You woke me up."

He lifted the helmet up. "Wanna go for a ride?"

"You have a motorcycle?" I rubbed my eyes and sighed as I turned back to the bed.

He stepped in front of me and sat on the bed before tugging me forward between his legs. He was so tall that even as he sat and I stood, we were at eye level. His large hands swallowed my waist, and I was accurately aware of their presence, each subtle movement alarming enough to clear my head.

116

I crossed my arms over my chest. "Are we just going to forget about the other night?"

"Yes, I have a bike," he said. "And no, we're not forgetting. I meant what I said."

When I didn't immediately answer, he tilted his head to the side and cocked a brow. I started to roll my eyes but stopped—then internally kicked myself for not doing it.

His one-sided smile deepened like he knew I'd silently followed his command. "Let's go for a ride. I know it's your off day."

"I haven't seen you with a bike."

"It's been at Grandma's house, but I moved it over here yesterday afternoon for this exact moment."

With a deep sigh, I rubbed my eyes again and spun to go to my closet.

He reclined on the bed, tucking his hands behind his head. "Is that a yes?"

I grinned at him over my shoulder as I pulled my oversized T-shirt off. "I guess so."

He watched me get ready before leading me outside. Parked on the front walkway was a blacked-out motorcycle and a second helmet sitting on the seat.

My feet slowed at the sight. "Are you sure?"

"Yep." He strolled past me down the stairs, nearly skipping. "Come on, little backpack."

My brows furrowed, and he laughed.

"Never mind," he said and extended a hand to me.

I smiled as curiosity got the best of me, and I slid my hand into his. "No, why did you call me that?"

"It's just a term for girls who ride as a passenger." He tugged me down the stairs toward the motorcycle. "They sit at the biker's back."

"Like a backpack," I finished for him, narrowing my

eyes. Although, the idea sounded...intriguing, to say the least. My eyes roamed over the bike as I walked around it. He handed me the extra helmet, and I pulled it on as he folded down the pegs on the back of the bike.

When he turned back to me, that devilish smirk returned."That is quite a good look on you."

Thank the Ghouls, he couldn't see my cheeks behind the tempered glass, because they were flaming. He pulled his own helmet on and turned away, kneeling down on one knee with his back to me.

"What?"

His helmet turned to me, and I couldn't see his face either. "Backpack?"

My mouth fell open as laughter bubbled in my chest. "You cannot be serious."

He braced a hand on his knee, his helmet cocking to the side. "Oh, come on." He held his hands out to the side, waiting. "Have a little fun."

I took a deep breath. "I'm going to regret this"

He shook his head. "I don't think so."

As I hopped on his back, he slid his hands under my knees and climbed onto the bike with ease. I released him and settled on the seat, bracing my feet on the pegs.

My stomach fluttered with nerves. If my poor heart beat, it'd be racing right now. "Have you done this before?"

"Nope." I could nearly hear his grin. "You'll be the first."

He grabbed my hands and wound them tightly around his waist. I loosened my hold to rest my hands on his hips, regaining a bit of space between us, but he grabbed my hands again and looped them around his waist.

"Is this necessary?" I asked as I sat back, placing my hands on his hips again. I needed space if I was going to breathe in anything other than his scent.

If I wanted to be able to *think*, I needed air—clean, plain air, untainted by the warmth and spice and mouth-watering dreams of what he could do with his mouth, of what I wanted to do with mine.

He shook his head and revved his bike. It jerked forward before stopping abruptly, and I was thrown into his back. His chest shook with a chuckle as my arms wrapped around his waist, and I released an annoyed huff.

"Ready?" His hand squeezed mine before moving to the handlebars.

My stomach flipped as I nodded.

He didn't waste a second. My scream was left at the Dead and Breakfast as we sped off down the road.

It was midday, and we'd been riding for hours.

I'd never smiled so much in my life. It was a gloriously free feeling after I relaxed into it, into him.

We drove down Sleepy Hollow Road now, a small back road that cut through the Sleepy Forest. It got its name from being calm and quiet—eerily so—but it was an other-worldly beauty. The brilliant orange and red leaves contrasted the gray sky beautifully, the crisp breeze rustling the trees.

This road was long, reaching from Hallow Falls all the way to...

I sat up straighter, my breath quickening.

"Where are we?" I whispered under my breath.

My head swiveled around, trying to study the area and the road behind us. It all looked the same. Air started to evade me, then I saw it.

The city limit sign.

Shaking my head, I tapped his chest. I tapped again and again and again, sitting back and pulling away from him as if that would prevent me from reaching the human realm any faster.

"What is it?" he asked, his voice laced with concern. He slowed the bike as he looked back at me.

The sign got bigger as we got closer.

"Jack!" I screamed.

The tires screeched to a halt, and we skidded sideways, stopping just before the city limit line.

I stumbled off the bike and landed on my hands and knees, vaguely hearing Jack's voice. My breaths were uneven and shallow, providing nothing but panic, my chest growing tighter. I jerked to my feet and ripped the helmet off, dropping it to the ground as I staggered back toward town. Tears poured down my cheeks.

"Remi, hey." Jack stepped in front of me, blocking my way as he leaned down, his eyes flitting back and forth between mine. "Hey, now. What's wrong?"

I pointed a finger back to the city limits when no words would come. His brows pulled together before understanding dawned on him.

"The humans." He cursed under his breath. "I'm sorry, Remi. I was thoughtless." His palms found my cheeks as he lifted my face to his, wiping them with his thumbs, and my head swam. "I didn't mean to scare you, baby."

A fresh wave of tears rolled down my cheeks as I clutched at my burning chest. Panic was a nasty beast; one I wished I didn't know so well.

"Match your breaths to mine." He inhaled slowly and exhaled slower. I tried to match his, but mine shook relentlessly. "Do it again." I inhaled slowly with him, holding his gaze. "Don't let the fear control you. You're safe."

We stood this way in the middle of the road for Ghouls knew how long. It could have been hours, days, weeks, but we didn't move an inch until the air returned to my lungs, then I laid my head on his chest, exhausted. He held me with his hand on the back of my head, smoothing my hair, his heartbeat steady beneath my ear. It was calming, and for a while, I just listened to the life beneath his warm skin.

"You're brave, Remi. I think..." he whispered, and I pulled back to look at him. "I think I need to be brave, too. Are you up for going to one more place? I swear to every god and ghoul listening, we won't go near the city limits again."

I glanced back, looking at the bike, at its proximity to those who would hunt me down again. I knew those men were dead; I'd killed those who had survived the night. But knowing that did nothing as my body seemed to forget, allowing the fear to take hold at the mere memory.

Swallowing hard, I turned back to him.

Don't let the fear control you.

"Fuck the fear, right?" I chuckled and wiped my swollen eyes.

"Right," he said, smiling wide. His eyes roamed over my face like he was checking me over. Seemingly satisfied, he kissed my forehead, and my lips parted in a slight gasp. "Stay right here. I'll go get the bike."

As he jogged back to it, my fingers touched where he'd kissed. It was different than every other time—gentle.

WE CREPT down the winding dirt road through Sleepy Forest.

It got darker and cooler the deeper we went, and a dull roar had started about a mile back.

I clutched to Jack as if he were the only thing keeping me upright. "Where are we going?"

"To the darkest part of Hallow Falls."

My chest clenched at his words, and I tightened my grip around his waist. He was forcing himself to face his demons. A warmth spread through my chest for him, something akin to pride.

A massive waterfall came into view. The trees' leaves around it were a deep blood red, their bark as black as midnight, and several pumpkin vines covered the ground, winding between them and growing the largest pumpkins I had ever seen. It was barely past midday, yet the area was as dark as late sunset, after the sun had already dipped below the horizon and the only remaining light was the final rays chasing after the sun.

The entire clearing was stuck in perpetual twilight.

After he parked the bike, he stepped off and grabbed my waist to lift me up and set me on my feet. I slid my hand into his, and he peeked down at me, lacing his fingers through mine.

"I don't want to be scared of my own damned magic." His steps slowed at the water's edge. "I always wanted to make Grandma proud and follow her in her footsteps. I wanted to be light. I wanted to be good."

My chest ached for him.

"You *are* good, Jack. You are kind and funny and brave." I shook my head with a breathy laugh. "You certainly have changed my life for the better, dark magic or not."

His brows furrowed, his chest rising and falling quickly.

A muscle feathered in his jaw before he shifted his gaze to the darkest part of the forest. The shadows deepened beneath it, the only color that of the blood-red leaves.

I stood on my toes, and he stilled when I placed a hand on his cheek to turn his face back toward me. His piercing blue irises were glowing now, I was sure of it—an unnatural blue, the color of icebergs lit with sunlight.

"If this is the magic you were meant to have, then it cannot harm you." I tapped his chest. "Not even here. It cannot control you."

He blinked rapidly, and his throat bobbed. "I know. I know you're right in theory, but it's pretty damn terrifying."

"I know." Both of my hands were on his cheeks now. I pulled him down and brushed my lips along his cheek as I whispered, "But we fuck the fear. Not the other way around."

His chest shook with a silent laugh before he planted a quick kiss on my cheek. "Fuck the fear."

With a deep breath, he pulled from my grasp and stepped toward the forest. At the shadows' edge, he glanced over his shoulder at me, and I nodded in encouragement.

No one's magic controlled them, but I understood his fear. No one else in Aggie's family had been beckoned to this side of magic—not that I knew of—but Aggie would never look down on him for this. She looked at a person's character, and Jack's was... Well, he was good, and she was proud. She should be.

"Be brave," I whispered, too quiet for him to hear, as he stepped into the shadows.

Hesitantly, he placed his palm on a black tree trunk, and his head fell back with a sigh. Shadows crawled over him from the bark and up from the ground. They consumed his form until they sank beneath his skin; he absorbed them.

He pulled his hand from the tree and held his arms to the side as more shadows slithered their way to him.

It was hauntingly beautiful to watch, stunningly terrifying as he welcomed the darkness. *Mesmerizing.*

A minute passed, and the darkness of the forest had faded a bit. When Jack opened his eyes to me, they were entirely black for a beat before dissipating into his normal blue. His grin was infectious as he jogged to me and scooped me up in a hug, spinning around.

I squealed, and he set me on my feet again.

"How do you feel?" I asked.

"Incredible, actually." He ran a hand through his hair. "I don't feel...different in the ways I thought I would. I feel like I just took a real breath of fresh air for the first time in my life, like every time before this had been only half breaths. Does that make any sense at all?"

"It makes perfect sense." I grabbed his cheeks again, pulling him down to me, and kissed his chin, his nose, his forehead. His laughter echoed all around us as he wound his arms around my waist. "I am so damn proud of you, Jack."

He pulled back, smiling softly. "Come on. Let's get out of here."

With that, he scooped me up again, and I wrapped my legs around his waist, giggling as he strode toward the bike.

18

PUMPKINS, ZOMBIES, & OTHER DELIGHTFUL THINGS

Eliza and I waved our slimy hands at Ambercup as he strolled by with a steaming paper cup in hand. He lifted it in greeting on his way to the wall of carved pumpkins.

The sounds of laughing children and happy chatter were louder than the Halloween music playing from the nearby speakers, and the scent of funnel cake and coffee drifted on the gentle breeze as the sun started to descend on the horizon.

"This fundraiser is always my favorite. The Scare School kids do such a good job on the pumpkin wall." Eliza beamed, dumping another scoop of pumpkin guts on the ground. "Did you hear our mysterious anonymous donor gave a hefty donation to this fundraiser as well? Another five grand."

My eyebrows shot to my hairline. "*Another* five grand? We've never had donors like this before."

"I know." She shrugged. "I wonder who it is."

I had a sneaking suspicion as only one newcomer had been roaming our little town this month, but it didn't seem feasible. I refused to believe it and definitely didn't want to sound like an idiot asking him if I was wrong. How would he have money like that? And why would he care that much about our fundraisers?

"Can you believe Halloween is in a week?" Eliza asked.

Usually, that statement would have had me bubbling with excitement, but this year, it felt forced. A small amount of disappointment had settled my chest, and I hadn't figured out why—or rather, I refused to look into it. I was afraid of the reasons I might find.

"Ghouls, no. I can't believe how fast October flew by this year." I lifted my small pumpkin to check if the triangle eyes were even; they were monstrously uneven. Rolling my eyes, I dropped it back to the ground and grabbed the carving tools again.

"I can't either," Eliza said as she grabbed the other carving knife. "So...who are you planning to ask to the Blood Ball?"

The Blood Ball was our annual masquerade ball. Every October 30th, we danced and drank until midnight to ring in Halloween together.

"Eddy, of course." I shook my head without pulling my eyes from my work. I carved the smaller triangle a bit larger, and when I was satisfied, I lifted it again. My mouth pressed into a flat line. It swapped; the smaller one was now the larger one. "I suck at this."

"Aw, no, it's cute," Eliza said as she turned the pumpkin toward her. "And you say that like it's obvious, but you've been dating them both. You seem pretty cozy with Jack from what I can tell." She wiggled her brows, biting her lip.

I set the pumpkin down, crossing my legs under me. "Yeah, well—"

"Mind if we join ya?" Aggie said, lugging her own

pumpkin that was three times larger than Jack's, who stood next to her with a ridiculous grin.

"Of course." I scooted over, so they could sit on the blanket with us.

Jack plopped down beside me and plucked the carving tool from my lap. "Yours is a bit lopsided."

I narrowed my eyes at him and shoved his shoulder. "Yeah. I know."

Aggie chuckled as she took to cutting a large circle around the stem. "Are you two going to the Zombies' Pub Crawl tonight?"

My mouth fell open, then snapped shut. Eddy had already asked me, but as I tried to tell her that, the shackle around my wrist burned, and Jack's hand found my thigh.

"Yes." I blinked rapidly, clearing my throat, and glanced up at Jack. "We are, aren't we?"

His mouth ticked up in his one-sided smile. He knew I'd have to cancel on Eddy, and his smug satisfaction made me want to throttle him.

"Wouldn't miss it." When the others were occupied with their work, he mouthed, "Good girl," and squeezed my thigh before patting it and turning back to his pumpkin.

My eyes were wide, my cheeks warm as I dropped my gaze back to the uneven triangles staring back at me.

FRED WAITED OUTSIDE of the first pub of the crawl, wearing his flannel and ironed jeans—his going-out clothes.

I patted him on the shoulder. "Who do you look so nice for tonight?"

He grinned and slowly wrapped an arm around my

shoulders, pulling me in for a hug. "Imogene is joining me on the crawl this evening."

"Aw, she is?" A smile stretched across my face. "That's amazing, Fred! I'm glad you finally asked her out. She deserves someone as kind as you."

He chuckled and released me. "But do I deserve her is the question. She is quite the beauty, that one."

"Of course, you do. You deserve each other." I patted him on the shoulder again. More zombies and pub crawl participants started to arrive, filing into our first stop. Country music drifted from inside; we were starting at the western bar. "I hope you two have a great night. Enjoy it."

His pale cheeks blushed a soft purple when his gaze landed on someone behind me, and his smile turned sheepish. He stepped around me and extended an elbow.

"Hi, Fred," Imogene said as she looped her arm through his, her expression beaming. She glanced at me, her white eyes lined with a deep violet eye shadow that matched the maxi dress she wore, and dipped her head in greeting. "Evening, Remi."

As Jack came into view with Aggie and Maggie, I excused myself to join them. Aggie and Maggie said hi but strolled on around me and into the bar. Jack hung back, and I furrowed my brows at him in confusion.

"What are we waiting for?" I hooked a thumb toward the entrance.

"Were you supposed to be here with Eddy tonight?"

A faint wave of guilt washed over me, and I dropped my eyes. "Yes, he asked me, but I told him never mind. I...lied." I scrunched my eyes. The word was bitter leaving my mouth. "I told him I decided to have a girl's night and just go with Aggie, Maggie, and Eliza."

"And you don't think he'll be here tonight? I just don't want Grandma to see anything she shouldn't."

I shook my head. "He doesn't usually attend the pub crawls. He likes to stick to his usual bar."

Jack's lips curved up, a devious glint in his eyes. "The one where my sweet, little angel couldn't keep her eyes off me?"

I rolled my eyes and stifled a smile, but my flushing cheeks gave me away. "That'd be the one."

He slid his hand into mine, our matching shackle marks tingling as they touched each other at our wrists, and tugged me toward the entrance.

Our smiles didn't falter from the moment we stepped inside the western bar to when we stepped out of the last pub in the crawl. The night was lighthearted and fun—exactly what I needed.

Eliza and Robert went home first, only halfway through the crawl, claiming they needed sleep, but I saw the heated glances they shared. Aggie was drunk by the time we made it to the last pub, stumbling and slurring her words, but she was so happy, it warmed my heart to see. She was clearly over the moon to spend so much time with Jack, and he reciprocated it, joking and teasing his grandmother, provoking a hilariously loud cackle from her each time.

Maggie shook her head, chuckling as she hooked her arm in Aggie's and led her down the street toward their apartment. They swayed as they strolled, Aggie singing an unintelligible song. Maggie gave us one last look, stifling her laugh as she waved goodbye.

As they disappeared out of sight, Jack turned to me, his eyes gleaming as a broad grin stretched across his face. I stepped into him, the alcohol making my own head fuzzy, and planted my hands on his chest. I tilted my face to his, and he lowered his to mine.

"Why are you staring at me like that?" I asked, cocking a brow in the same infuriating way he always did.

"I was just thinking that tonight was one of the best nights I've had in a long time," he whispered, tucking a strand of hair behind my ear.

My stomach flipped, but I shrugged nonchalantly, although I was sure my smirk revealed my thoughts. Drunk me was not good at hiding anything—clearly. "It was all right."

"All right?" He slid his palm onto my cheek, his chest shaking with a silent laugh. "If this is what you consider all right, I can't wait to see what you consider great."

"You think we'll have another night?"

His grip tightened on my cheek as he groaned and brushed his lips along my cheek, dangerously close to my lips. "God, I hope so."

My chest clenched, and I sucked in a breath as he moved his hand to the back of my head, knotting his fingers in my hair. I moaned as he kissed down my jaw to my neck and backed me against the outside wall of the pub. When my back hit the wall, his free hand grabbed my waist, holding me against him. I arched into his chest as he slid his tongue up the hollow of my throat.

Ghouls, I just want to kiss his lips. His lips to kiss me. Just one taste.

His mouth moved higher, skimming along my jaw. One small movement would send us over the edge, everything I wanted mere inches away.

My head swam.

Would it really be so bad to have these marks? Would it—

Suddenly, Jack jerked back. I gasped, opening my eyes to find Eddy ripping Jack off of me.

"What the hell?" Eddy shouted.

"Woah, man. Calm down," Jack said, holding his hands up. "This is not the time or place."

Eddy's eyes flashed to me, and my gut sank. Hurt swirled behind his outward anger.

"Eddy... I..."

"Is he who you ditched me for?" he asked. I shook my head, stuttering, and he tilted his head to the side, his eyes widening. "Is he?"

"Yes." The word tasted like poison on my tongue, and I wanted to vomit. I didn't want to hurt anyone; I never meant to. "I'm sorry, Eddy. You don't understand. We struck a—"

"No." Eddy stepped back and shook his head. "No, I'm the fool. I knew you were taking your time, seeing both of us, but I didn't think you'd blow *me* off for the asshole who'll be gone in a week."

"Hey, that's a bit much," Jack said, and Eddy swiveled to him, his werewolf eyes flashing yellow. "Remi doesn't deserve that."

"And who are you to say that?" Eddy stepped into Jack. "You just blew into town like a fucking tornado and now you think you know her? Can speak for her?"

"I know her well enough to know that I wouldn't pass her up for ten fucking years. You had *ten years*. Do you even understand how long that is?" Jack said. "Look at her, Eddy, really look at her. She's beautiful, kind, and by far the most compassionate person I've ever met. She should've given up on you years ago. You're fucking *blessed* she even gave you a chance after all this time."

Eddy clenched his jaw and his fists, the corded muscles twitching in his forearms.

"Jack..." I whispered, reaching for his arm. He stepped out of my grasp, and I swallowed hard. "Eddy, please. I didn't mean to hurt you. I would never want to hurt anyone."

Eddy chuckled, shaking his head as he stared at me for a beat before turning his gaze back to Jack. "You don't deserve her, Jack. You're just...sad. Coming into *my* town and trying to steal what was mine right from under my nose. Honestly, I don't even know what she sees in you."

Rage pulsed through me, and my teeth bared at Eddy as a newfound clarity poured over me like ice water.

Jack smiled—a terrifyingly vicious grin that held no mirth. "That's because I haven't fucked you."

My mouth snapped open at the same second Eddy's fist connected with Jack's jaw.

I smelled the blood before I saw it. It dribbled from Jack's busted lip, and he wiped it with his thumb, smiling as the red smeared across his skin. My lips parted as my gaze locked on it, my canines extending.

Jack laughed under his breath and stepped up to Eddy, but they both stilled as my hand found Jack's cheek. I pulled him toward me in a daze—that delicious red liquid trickling down his chin the only thing I could see. The only thing I could smell or think about.

Nothing else existed at this moment. Nothing, no one. Just the blood and its warm, spicy scent calling me like a moth to a flame.

I tugged him down and stood on my tiptoes to run my tongue over his skin, trailing from his chin to his lips. An audible moan left me, and I didn't care; it didn't matter. Nothing mattered but this. I sucked on his lower lip where it was split, and warmth flowed from it. He groaned into my mouth as he wound an arm around my waist, holding me against his chest.

"What the fuck?"

That snapped me out of it. I gasped and staggered back. Shame. Embarrassment. Anger. So many things bombarded me at once as my gaze darted back and forth between Eddy and Jack.

I licked my lips, tasting the remnants of Jack, and fought the urge to run back to him as a new dark droplet formed on his bruising lip.

"This..." I shook my head, stumbling away from them. "I'm sorry. I... I have to go."

I strode down the street as my eyes stung. Jack called after me, but I walked faster, wrapping my arms around myself.

Tears soaked my cheeks when I finally stepped into Shadow Park.

19

BEAT MY STILL HEART...OR IS IT THE OTHER WAY AROUND?

I spent the night in Ambercup's hut, huddled on a cot next to his fireplace.

He listened to me vent for hours, let me cry on his bony shoulder, and then firmly declared he was team Jack before I left with the sunrise, the morning especially cold on my walk back to the Dead and Breakfast. My breath came out in soft puffs of white, but I tightened Amber's coat around me and took my time, taking the longest possible route back.

The house was still quiet when I snuck in the front door and slipped into my room. After softly clicking the door closed, I turned and yelped. Jack sat on the edge of my bed, his shoulders slumped and mouth bruised, the crack in his lip scabbed. Dark circles had settled beneath his eyes like he hadn't closed them since I'd left.

"I'm sorry," he said, his voice defeated. "I'm sorry, Remi, for everything."

I clamped my mouth shut. I wasn't sure it was an apology I wanted. I didn't know what I wanted, so I said nothing at all. In my closet, I pulled off Amber's jacket and last night's clothing and tossed them in the laundry basket. I tugged on an oversized T-shirt, my thickest sweatpants, and a pair of fuzzy socks, hoping they would chase away the chill that had settled in my bones at some point last night.

With a deep sigh, I turned back to my room and found Jack standing in the closet doorway.

"I don't want to pretend anymore." His words were quiet, honest, and pulled at my heartstrings.

But he was leaving. Soon. And we hurt Eddy, someone I cared for deeply. Whether I chose to be with Eddy after this didn't matter; he was still a friend, a *person*, and we hurt him.

I tugged at the bottom of my T-shirt, keeping my gaze on the floor. "You told Eddy we 'fucked.'"

He stepped forward and slid a finger under my chin. "I'm sorry, baby, so fucking sorry."

"I don't..." I stepped back from him, putting space between us again.

"I shouldn't have said that. I was angry. I just... That imbecile doesn't own you. No one does." He ran a hand through his dark hair. "But it wasn't my place, I know that, and I'm sorry."

I bit the inside of my cheek. This was too much. He was leaving, for Ghouls' sake. Why did it even matter? Why did he have to be this close, apologizing like it hurts him, too? This whole thing—me, him, this arrangement—was nothing but a deal.

"You're just..." Frustration boiled in my gut. This was pointless, all of it. My heart hurt, and for what? I scoffed and shook my head as I shoved past him. He swiveled on his heel and followed close behind me.

"Talk to me, Remi." He closed his fingers around my

wrist and swiveled me back to him. His brows furrowed over his blue eyes, worry pressing between them.

My throat bobbed. "I don't want this. I don't want...you."

His face jerked back as if I'd slapped him.

If he was going to leave, I wanted him gone now. I didn't want to drag this out so that he could wind his fingers further around my naive heart. I wasn't going to let him take it with him when he left us all behind.

"You lie," he hissed, clenching his teeth. "Have you truly not realized that I have the same sense as Aggie? I can taste your bitter little lies on my tongue, Remi."

My eyes widened as the puzzle pieces fell together before my eyes. Of course, he had the same sense. I should've expected it, but it changed nothing.

I dropped my eyes to my hands, now knotted in my T-shirt—my pathetic attempt at holding myself together. "No."

He gripped my chin between his thumb and forefinger to turn me back to him. "If you're going to lie to me, then you're going to look me in the eye while you do it."

I inhaled slowly, committing his scent to memory as I breathed it in for the last time. My eyes burned as I held his gaze, his face blurred behind rising tears. I blinked them away, and one slid down my cheek. "I don't want you."

He dropped his hand, a muscle feathering in his jaw. "I thought we were done with fear, baby. Fuck the fear, was it?" He took a step back and then another before grabbing his leather jacket from the bed. His eyes found me once more, roaming over my form as he shook his head. "What a load of bullshit. You're letting nothing *but* fear control you."

My breath hitched as he strode out the door and shut it behind him. I stared at it as I fell to my knees, feeling my still heart crack for the first time. Before this month, it'd been so long since I'd felt anything where I knew it should be that I'd begun to question its existence, but now...

Now, its presence was more known than anything I had ever felt. It was a breath-sucking devastation; one I never imagined could be so painful.

20

HELL WEEK

Some people dubbed the week before Halloween "Hell Week" as the preparations for our biggest holiday of the year were endless, and the influx of people could double the town's occupancy on a good year.

But the term felt especially accurate this time around.

My chest still ached, my breath leaving me at random times. Jack was gone, either staying somewhere else or gone from town entirely. I didn't ask; I hadn't even seen Aggie. Just making breakfast each morning for my rapidly growing list of guests took everything I had, much less volunteering at the Books and Boos.

The Dead and Breakfast was fully booked for the night, including Jack's old room. It hurt to give the key to the new guests—a happy vampire couple—but I forced myself to book it. He was gone, moving on, and I needed to do the same. This felt like the first step.

Well, actually, the first step was opening the window to rid the room of his scent. I'd cried doing that, too. Stupid, ridiculous tears over a stupid, ridiculous situation.

Now, I was cuddled up on the bay window beneath a

soft blanket, surrounded by pumpkins, mums, and sunflowers, watching the raindrops slide down the window when Amber walked into the kitchen.

His hollow smile had fallen, the flickering light inside his pumpkin head dim. "How are you doing, champ?"

"I'm fine, why?" I moved a few things around to make room for him as he strolled over.

He sighed and sat beside me, reclining his head on the window. "You're not fine, Remi." My heart sank, my brows furrowing. I opened my mouth to speak, but he continued. "I've known you for a *very* long time, and I've never seen you like this. You're heartbroken."

Heartbroken. For some unfathomable reason, hearing him say the word set loose a wave of emotion inside me like I hadn't already known that. Maybe I hadn't, but it was true. I was heartbroken over someone I'd known for less than a month.

"It's ridiculous." I chuckled, even though my throat was tight and a tear escaped my eye. I quickly wiped it away. "Stupid and ridiculous."

"It's not stupid or ridiculous," he whispered. I turned to him, and his carved brows were down turned. "It's not. He brought out a side of you I've never seen. Even if things didn't end up the way you expected... None of this is ridiculous."

I choked, my breath hiccuping. "I don't know how to feel."

He laughed and pulled me into a hug. "You're not supposed to know how to feel, Remi. Nothing about love ever makes sense; there's no use in trying to decipher what it should or shouldn't be."

I stilled. "Love?"

"Why, yes, love," he said, as if it were obvious.

Is that...Is that what this is?

I didn't answer him after that as I let the question echo in my mind. We sat this way for a while, listening to the pitter-patter of rain, but when it finally lightened up, lessening to a drizzle, he released me.

I exhaled slowly and sat up. "I suppose I should go see Aggie."

"She would like that very much. She misses you." He stood and extended an elbow.

We strolled to Books and Boos together, and when it came into view, a bundle of nerves settled in my stomach. The bell jingled overhead as we entered, the scent of coffee, apples, and old books welcoming me back like an old friend. I inhaled deeply, allowing the familiar scent to calm my frayed nerves, as the door shut with a click, and the rain picked back up, the soft roar drowning out the music playing.

Aggie stuck her head out from behind a bookshelf. "Oh, thank the Ghouls. It's about damn time, child."

As Aggie lifted her velvet skirt and jogged over, Amber gave her two thumbs up. "I delivered one sad vampire. As promised."

My face whipped to him, my mouth agape.

Aggie threw her arms around me in a tight hug. "I asked him to bring you. I was so damned worried." She pulled back and swatted my shoulders. "How could ya leave me so worried?"

"I'm sorry. I should've come in and helped. I—"

She swatted me again, harder.

"Aggie!"

"Do you really think it's your help I care about? I was worried about *you*, Remi." She led me to her table and chairs. As we sat, she took my hands in hers. "Jack told me what happened."

She flipped my hand, and I realized she was looking at the shackle mark on my wrist. Understanding dawned on me, and my damned eyes watered again. *When were they going to run out of tears?*

"I see your mark has become visible, too," she whispered, her eyes flicking up to meet mine as she released my hand. She stood and walked to the nearby stand where she kept her cider. After filling a steaming cup, she pulled out a flask from Ghouls knows where and poured a heavy shot in, then slid it across the table to me as she sat back in her chair, the old wood creaking under her.

"He... He still has his mark, too?" I asked, hesitant, anticipating the pain that crawled into my chest.

She nodded slowly. "You both broke the deal. It's not going anywhere, child."

My breath left me in a whoosh, my brows drawing together.

A permanent reminder.

A faint wisp of regret passed through me; if the marks were going to be permanent, I wished I would've kissed him. At least then it would have felt worth it.

"How is he?"

"He's...alive," she said. "The poor fool has been sleeping on my couch."

My eyes flashed to her. "He didn't leave?"

"Ghouls, no. He's barely left the couch, much less left town."

I swallowed hard, suddenly thankful we hadn't run into him on the way here. Tomorrow was Halloween, then he would be gone, and I would never have to worry about it again.

I rubbed at my permanent shackle mark, now visible to the rest of the world. Well, at least, I wouldn't have to *see* him again.

"But he'll have to leave on the first, either way. His next tour starts two states over on the third."

My head tilted to the side. "Tour?"

"He didn't tell you about his book tour? That surprises me," she said with a soft laugh. "He's a pretty well-known paranormal author, been on the *New York Times* Best Seller's list more times than I can count. His next book is set to release in November; hence, the book tour."

My jaw was on the floor. I knew it was, but I couldn't help it. "What?"

"He really didn't tell you?"

I shook my head as I reclined back in the chair, stunned.

"Well, while I'm spoiling secrets..." She paused before throwing her hands up. "Hell, he's my grandson. I can brag if I want to. He's also the town's anonymous donor. He's donated at least five grand to every fundraiser this month."

My hands fell to my lap as I stared at her. I was at a loss for words. "What?"

Do I know any other words?

"Yep." She nodded and lifted her mug to her lips, blowing softly. "He's not such a bad guy."

"No," I whispered, my eyes unfocused as they dropped to the table between us. *I never thought he was. Quite the opposite, in fact.*

21

THE GHOULS-FORSAKEN BLOOD BALL, FOLLLOWED BY...

My heart wasn't in it.

Not as Eliza curled my hair and did my makeup. Not as I pulled on the blood-red silk gown and Eliza tied up the back strings. Not as my makeshift family and I walked together downtown. Not as we ascended the entryway stairs and handed the doorman our tickets.

Not even as we stepped into the Blood Ball—my favorite tradition of all time.

Nothing about this event appealed to me. I wanted to go home and crawl into bed. To rip this silly, frivolous fabric from my body, toss it into the trash, and wrap myself in a million blankets.

I'd bought this dress maybe a week after Jack had arrived with absolutely no intention of him ever seeing it. He wasn't even a passing thought in regards to the ball, but now...

Now, I was subconsciously looking for him everywhere I went, constantly on edge, and tonight was no different. Eddy had faded into the background entirely. How had I been so oblivious to my growing feelings for Jack? They had snuck up on me, hiding behind my shallow feelings for Eddy.

But his absence was a constant ache—one I hoped plagued him as well so at least then, I wouldn't be alone in the hurt. It was selfish but true all the same.

We stepped inside the ballroom, and Eliza grabbed my hand, giving it a quick squeeze.

The large room, surrounded by an overlooking balcony, was lit with a soft, flickering light, the candelabras and chandeliers all holding small flames. Fall garlands had been hung along the walls and rails while bouquets of dark red roses and sunflowers were placed on every table. It was dark and romantic as it always was.

My chest clenched, and I made a beeline for the bar.

I ordered a strong drink—bartender's choice—and sipped from it, trying not to cringe at the taste when Maggie stepped into my peripheral vision. I turned to her as she leaned on her elbows and stuck a finger up to the bartender.

Her eyes twinkled when she glanced at me. "I told you this month would be a little sweeter."

It took me a moment to process her words, but when they hit, bitterness curled in my stomach. "Sweeter?" I asked, rolling my eyes as I turned my attention to the shelves of alcohol along the back wall.

"Yes, I would say sweeter," she hummed.

I opened my mouth to reply, but she pointed to the other side of me. Turning, I found Aggie reclining on her elbows.

"This feels suspiciously like an intervention or an interrogation or..." My gaze shot back and forth between them.

"Or something. Look, I really don't want to talk about it. About any of it."

"Do you love Jack?" Aggie asked calmly.

My face swiveled to her. Surely I hadn't heard her correctly. "What?"

"Do you. Love. Jack?" Her gaze was curious, searching but not prying or invasive.

I stared at her. The words set off a wave of adrenaline that poured through my veins like liquid fire. I didn't know what to say or how to answer; I wasn't even sure I wanted to admit anything to myself, much less to them.

"Do not lie to me, child. Much like my grandson, I can taste lies." She narrowed her eyes at me, searching my face for her answer. When she found what she was looking for, her face fell—not in shock but awe. "You do, don't you?"

A faint ghost of a smile curved her lips. My mouth fell open and snapped shut again, my cheeks burning.

"Don't you?" she asked again, softer this time, gentle.

"Yes," I breathed, the word barely audible.

She nodded once and ruffled through her purse before shoving a pair of car keys into my hands. "Then, you must go. He's on his way out of town right now."

Something deep in my chest lurched, my breathing quickening. I held the keys but didn't move.

"Either go get him," Maggie said, "or you're letting him go, because I have a feeling he won't be coming back. Not with the way things are now."

My eyes shot to her as panic surged. *Do I want him to come back?*

I bit my lip, my eyes falling to the wooden bar. *Can I live without ever seeing him again? Without ever hearing his voice or feeling his touch?*

I curled my fingers around Aggie's keys. There was a

fine line between living and merely surviving, and I was tired of tip-toeing it.

I want to live. My chest clenched, and I hopped off the bar stool. *I want Jack.*

I took a hesitant step back. "Thank you. Thank you both."

Aggie climbed onto the bar stool I was sitting on. I held her gaze for a beat, and she smiled, waving her hands in an encouragement to go. With a deep, shaky inhale, I turned and sprinted past everyone, down the stairs into the parking lot. There I found Aggie's small car parked illegally in front of the sidewalk.

My eyes brimmed with tears as I laughed and threw the door open to climb in. I jammed the key in the ignition and turned. It made a clicking noise but nothing happened.

"Oh, no." I tried again. Nothing. "No, no, no."

Rain started to fall, and I cursed, hitting the steering wheel with my palm.

Closing my eyes, I inhaled slowly and tried again. The car clicked over and over with a worrisome whirring noise. I turned the key back and took another slow breath.

I am coming for you, Jack, with or without this damned car.

Silently praying to the Ghouls, I tried again, and by some miracle, it cranked. The old car shook hard enough to rattle my bones, but a relieved laugh escaped me. I shifted into drive and pulled out of the parking lot much faster than was appropriate, earning a few nasty looks.

I made my way down Sleepy Hollow Road, the windshield wipers going as fast as they could as rain pelted down. When the city limits sign came into view, my chest tightened, but I pushed down on the gas.

It was his voice that whispered in my mind: *Fuck the fear.*

My knuckles were white as I gripped the steering wheel, and the engine roared as I accelerated right past the city limit and into the human realm, leaving Hallow Falls in the rear view mirror.

Three miles later, I saw it. Parked under the sole street lamp was a black bike and its rider seated at the base of the pole, sitting in the rain. My eyes burned again. I swerved onto the side of the road and threw the car in park.

In the torrential downpour, I ripped the door open and stumbled out.

22
CONFESSIONS

I slammed the car door shut and ran to Jack, my heels clicking on the concrete.

Sinking to my knees in front of him, I placed my palms on either side of his face and lifted his gaze to me.

His eyes were red, his hair and clothes soaked. "What are you..." His eyes roamed over my body as the drenched ruby fabric clung to me, and a sad smile curved his lips. His next words were barely audible as he whispered, "An angel on Earth."

My breath hitched as tear after tear slid free, getting lost in the falling rain. My sopping hair clung to my face, and he tucked it behind my ears before he leaned his forehead onto mine, holding onto me like he was afraid I would disappear.

"I don't want to pretend," I whispered. He stilled, but his chest rose and fell quickly. "I don't want to pretend that this wasn't the best month of my entire life. I don't want to pretend that I'm okay with you leaving. I don't..." A choked sound cut off my words, and he tightened his grip. "I don't want to pretend that I'm not in love with you."

He pulled back, his blue eyes searching my face, his dark brows furrowed.

"I couldn't leave you, Remi." He brushed his lips along my cheek. "I made it this far, and my heart, my *soul*, refused to go another foot, another inch, away from you." His hand found the nape of my neck. "I love you. With everything that I am and everything that I will ever be, I love you."

Then, his lips slid along mine for the first time, shattering the remnants of my self-control. A sob broke from me, and he swallowed the sound, deepening the kiss and sending a wave of satisfying warmth through me.

I crawled into his lap and straddled him, my palms on his cheeks holding him to me so he could never leave. I never wanted space again. I never wanted air. All I wanted was this: Jack's lips on mine because it felt so *right*.

Everything about him and us and this night was right.

It was in this moment, lost to him and his touch, that I realized every single thing that had ever gone wrong in my life was only a stepping stone to lead me here, to him, to this.

I smiled into his mouth, and his arms tightened around my waist.

No, nothing had ever gone wrong at all. Every step, every choice, every disappointment... All a part of the path that led me to Jack, and I knew in the very depths of my soul that I would retrace every single damned step in every life if I thought it would lead me to him again and again.

It was worth it. *He* was worth it.

We kissed like two people starved of touch, deprived and finally within reach of satiation—because we *were*. A very long month without a true kiss had left us ravenous, and Ghouls be damned if I wasn't going to make up for it right here and now.

We were both soaked to the bone, but my chest had never felt warmer. It swelled and swelled, and I feared I might fly if it grew any lighter.

But then, a thump sounded in my chest.

I sucked in a breath and pressed a hand to my sternum.

"What is it?" he asked, concern furrowing his brows.

Another thump.

A cry wracked my body as I lifted his hand to my throat, placing his fingers along the hollow. Another thump, and his eyes widened.

He smirked, moving his hand to my jaw and pulling me back down to his lips. "Does this mean your heart beats for me?"

I giggled and wrapped my arms around his neck as I kissed his cheeks, his nose, his forehead, his *lips*. "It was always you."

His smile deepened, revealing his dimple, and I kissed that, too, as I would a hundred more times. A thousand.

Every day for the rest of our very long lives.

COMPLETELY UNNECESSARY
BUT TOTALLY FUN BONUS
CHAPTER

DECEMBER 31ST

The full moon was bright overhead, snow crunching underfoot as I sprinted through the Sleepy Forest. Fireworks cracked in the distance, temporarily lighting the forest in a rainbow of colors before plunging us back into darkness.

Heavy footsteps behind me urged my legs to move faster, adrenaline pouring through my veins as laughter bubbled in my chest. He was gaining ground somehow—probably cheating with that dark magic of his.

Jack's magic had flared a new desire in him. He wanted to chase. When he'd first told me, I was hesitant, but I couldn't deny the thrill it spiked in me—another alluring depravity to add to our growing list.

This wasn't our first time, but it was no less exhilarating. Each time helped me heal in some weird, twisted way. I wasn't scared of the dark or running anymore, because I knew exactly who was behind me and who would capture me when I was too tired to go any farther.

We were fucking the fear...and each other. I laughed aloud and slapped a hand over my mouth as the sound echoed through the silent forest over my footsteps.

Now as I ran with everything I had, I was burning—muscles, lungs, and especially my core, but not with fear or panic. It was entirely lust and excitement.

I didn't expect to love it so much, but Ghouls, I did. It was electrifying, the icy air contrasting my heated skin as he slowly closed the distance between us.

But I wasn't going to make it easy on him.

If he wanted to catch and conquer his prey, he would have to work for it. I wanted him on edge and unleashed when he finally caught me, so he would take out every delicious urge on my body without restraint.

Biting my lip, smiling so hard my cheeks hurt, I pushed my feet harder, and his deep laugh surrounded me. The clearing with Jack's waterfall was just ahead; the area would be warm, as the ground magically stayed the same temperature year-round—a crisp sixty degrees, but anything was better than the frigid twenty it was out here.

Satisfaction filled me when the clearing came into view, the roaring of the waterfall permeating the silence. I took one step into the warmth, and Jack grabbed my wrist and spun me toward him. I gasped, not having noticed how close he was, and hit his chest.

He didn't give me a breath before crashing his mouth to mine with a groan, his hands on either side of my face. I pressed my body into him as I wrapped my arms around his neck, pulling him ever closer to me. He was never close enough.

He walked me back into a tree and released my face to unzip my jacket, sliding it off before dropping it to the ground, not missing a beat with his mouth which now seared a path down my neck to my shoulder. He bit *hard* and ripped my shirt off—literally ripped. I sucked in a breath as the chilled air hit my bare breasts, but his warm mouth covered one while his hand found the other.

I arched against the tree, my fingers knotted in his hair as he flicked and swirled his tongue over my sensitive nipple. His free hand shoved my jeans down, and I stepped out of them as he ripped my underwear off, too, tearing the small strings of the thong.

When I was entirely bare, Jack stepped back, letting his gaze pour over my form. It didn't matter how many times we did this, how many times we had sex, he *always* stopped to appreciate first. I loved it, more than I probably should— our special form of foreplay, his gaze nearly tangible on my skin, or perhaps it was his shadows accompanying it, trailing over me like a tease.

His shadow magic had been a stunning addition to the rest of him, and it took him no time at all to learn how to use it—a skill I was immensely grateful for, especially right now as a dark, translucent hand slipped between my thighs.

My head fell back as his low laugh filled my ears.

One shadowed hand teased along my core, pulling a moan from my lips, as another slid a finger up my spine, matching the pace of the one skimming up my front between my breasts. When they both rose above my neck, the back one knotted in my hair, the front gripping my cheek.

"I'll never not be rendered speechless by your beauty, little monster," Jack whispered, his words caressing me in the way they always did. He stepped forward, and his hand replaced the shadow on my cheek as he brushed his lips against mine. It was sweet and gentle, but not for long, quickly turning hungry.

He wasn't alone in that hunger; it swept through me just as harshly, an insatiable need to taste him.

I moaned as his tongue and shadow fingers entered me simultaneously. He groaned in approval, his warm hand gripping my waist as he pulled me into him. My bare body met his clothed one, and my fingers fumbled with the buttons along his shirt. He smiled against my mouth, letting me clumsily undress him.

After I slid his shirt from his shoulders and tossed it, I unbuckled his belt and slid it from the loops. It fell to the ground with a soft clank as I unbuttoned his pants, but before I could remove them, he slipped a finger under my chin and forced my gaze back to his.

"Tell me, baby, do you remember what I asked all those months ago? When I asked what—or rather, *who* you'd think of while this sweet, little pussy rode Eddy's dick?"

My breath hitched, brows furrowed, but I nodded.

"We have company, little monster."

The words sent a shock through me, my heart skipping a beat, but the look on his face was devilish, his smirk revealing that dimple in his cheek. I swallowed hard and followed his gaze over my shoulder.

Stepping from the woods on the opposite side of the clearing was an overgrown wolf with burning amber eyes.

Jack carefully, slowly, stepped in front of me, shielding most of my naked form, and I peeked my head around him.

"Ed," Jack called.

Eddy blinked once before backing into the darkness of the tree line. When he came forward again, he was human —naked but human, his eyes still a glowing yellow.

I didn't bother averting my gaze, even as my cheeks flushed furiously.

Nobody said a word for a few beats, but the tension… The tension in the air was thick enough to cut with a knife but not malicious.

No, it was expectant, heated, and *rising*.

Jack tilted his head to the side. "My offer to share still stands." Eddy's eyes flared and darted to me. Jack glanced down at me, too, cocking a brow. "If Remi wants to."

My mouth parted, a small breath hitching as my gaze shifted from Jack to Eddy and back. I smiled faintly, every deep, depraved part of me awakening with my fangs as they slid from my gums. They peeked over my red-lined lips and didn't go unnoticed. Jack's eyes dropped to the two points, and he grinned.

"Say the words, little monster," he whispered, low enough that only I could hear.

"I want to share," I whispered, and his smile deepened before he turned to Eddy.

Placing a hand on my lower back, Jack stepped from in front of me and gently guided me forward. Eddy's gaze fell to my breasts first before dipping lower, seeing parts of me no one else ever had—save for Jack.

The lust in Eddy's gaze lifted my chin higher. While he was a solid foot taller than me, I still felt like I was looking down my nose at him; perhaps this was the night he would fall to his knees before me.

My mouth ticked up as I stepped toward him.

"You want to touch her, Eddy?" Jack whispered, standing at my back. "Taste her? Have her?"

Eddy's eyes flashed to Jack, and he ran a hand over the scruff along his chin, his jaw clenching. "More than anything."

Eddy lifted a hand to my waist, sliding higher, and Jack knotted his hand in my hair to pull me back. I stumbled a step and glanced at Jack, confused but *deeply* aroused.

Jack's heated gaze was locked on Eddy.

"Beg." My heart skipped a beat, but Jack's tone left no room for argument, no questioning. "Beg her for a touch, Ed. Beg her for a taste." Jack swiveled me to him and crashed his mouth to mine, thrusting his tongue in my mouth with a groan that had me arching into his chest. When he pulled back, I was left in a daze, blinking rapidly. "Because God, she tastes *damn* good."

My body was burning, my lips parted and head swimming, when Jack gripped me by the nape of my neck and turned me back to Eddy, walking me forward at arm's length.

When I stood right in front of him, Eddy's mouth curved up in a one-sided grin. "Beg?"

"Beg," I repeated.

Jack stood at my back, one of his hands splaying across my abdomen, another over my left breast. Eddy's eyes fell and his mouth followed, hanging open—it must have been Jack's shadows caressing me. When Eddy met my gaze again, his yellow irises glowed like the moon.

"Please, Remi." His voice was low, undercut with a growl that wasn't normally there. He stepped closer, his hands hovering over my skin but not touching. "Please let me touch you... Kiss you..." His face lowered to mine, and a shadow hand tipped my chin back so that Eddy's lips were mere inches from mine as he whispered, "Let me taste you."

My eyes dropped to his mouth before rising back to his eyes, and I nodded. He didn't waste a second. One large hand wrapped around my lower back and pulled me into him while the other gripped my face, his mouth claiming mine. It wasn't soft. No, this was pure lust.

He walked me back a step, and my body pressed into Jack, his form warm and solid as Eddy's mouth devoured me. Shadows and solid hands covered me, every inch being touched in some way.

A finger dipped into my soaked core, and I moaned into Eddy's mouth, who growled in return. Jack's hand slid over my shoulder, pulling my hair back, and I broke from Eddy's to turn between them. Wrapping my arms around Jack's neck, I pulled him down to me and kissed him like a starved woman, leaning back into Eddy's muscular chest.

Eddy's hands roamed over my body, my hips, my waists, my breasts. As he circled his fingers around my nipples, I moaned, letting my head fall back on his chest.

Jack smiled, reveling in my every reaction as he leaned forward to nip my lower lip. "She's such a good, little monster, huh, Ed?"

"Fucking perfect," he growled, and I gasped as he pinched my nipples and ground his hardened length against my backside.

Good Ghouls, what have I gotten myself into?

Jack leaned into my ear to whisper, "I can feel how soaked you are already, baby. You're so fucking needy, aren't you? So desperate for both of us?"

My breath hitched, and I nodded, breathless as one of their fingers continued to slide in and out of me, moving faster. It slipped out, and I nearly mourned the loss, but two more entered. My moan rang out in the empty clearing.

"Then, I need you to be a good girl and take Eddy's cock. Your pussy is a fucking *blessing,* baby. Let the man have a taste of heaven."

"Oh, Ghouls," I breathed, but I stilled when Jack's hand wrapped around Eddy's throat.

We stood still as stone as they locked eyes, the only movement that of Jack's fingers still curling inside me and my chest rising and falling in pants.

"But know this, Ed, Remi *is* mine. Got it?"

A muscle feathered in Eddy's jaw as he nodded. "Got it."

With that, Jack's normal ease returned, and he released Eddy's throat to wrap a hand around the back of my head. He reclaimed my mouth, thrusting his tongue in as he pulled his hand from between my legs, trailing the wetness along my hip, but his fingers were quickly replaced with Eddy's.

"Ghouls," I moaned again, and Jack smiled against my lips.

He gave me a quick peck on the lips, then my nose before pulling back slightly. Resting a hand on each of my shoulders, he gently pushed me down, and I dropped to my knees between them. They both lowered on either side of me as Eddy placed a hand between my shoulder blades. He pushed me forward until I was on my hands and knees, slapping my ass with a groan.

Jack slid a finger under my chin to tilt my face up, his gaze peering into my soul as he asked, "Are you sure about this?"

"Yes." I nodded fiercely. *Ghouls, yes.*

He smiled with such pride that my chest swelled as he splayed his fingers across my cheek and leaned down to kiss me. I gasped into his mouth as Eddy slid the tip of his cock along my entrance.

"So wet," Eddy growled and gripped my waist with one large hand, holding me in place. Jack covered my mouth with his as Eddy slowly pushed inside me, and I moaned into Jack, my brows furrowing, my fingers digging into the dirt. Eddy was *big*, stretching me wide. "So perfect."

He pulled out slowly to thrust back in harder. I broke from the kiss with a scream, throwing my head back. Eddy wrapped my hair around his fist and unleashed himself—a merciless pace that threw me into a frenzy.

"You're doing such a good job, taking him so beautifully," Jack said as he finished unbuttoning his pants. My eyes followed, my mouth watering as they slid to the ground, and he stepped out of them, freeing his length. He dropped to his knees in front of me, running the tip of his cock along my lips. "Don't bite, baby."

I opened dutifully, gratefully, and he slid into my mouth with a groan. His lips parted, his eyes locked on me, as he pushed deeper until he hit my throat. He sat here, holding my head still, cutting my air off, smiling down at me, for a few, very long seconds before pulling back an inch. I sucked in a sharp breath, bobbing on him from the motion of Eddy behind me.

"God, you are so fucking beautiful," Jack said and thrust into my mouth. He hit the back of my throat and didn't stop, immediately pulling out and pushing back in. His head fell back as he fucked my mouth, my eyes watering.

Then, a hand reached under me to the apex of my thighs. I moaned around Jack, a tear slipping free from my eye. The pleasure was too much—it was all too much. My nerves were on frayed, and the swirling over my clit was going to kill me.

Another hand pinched my nipple, and a sob broke from my throat. I was being assaulted on all fronts—my core, my clit, my mouth, my nipple.

Another hand found my other nipple.

Too much. Too much. Too much.

When a finger found my ass, I lost it, my entire body quivering. If not for Eddy holding me up, I'm sure my body would have betrayed me and fallen to the ground. The finger slid inside, and I released a trembling moan, my back arching as they both pounded into me relentlessly, edging me closer and closer to orgasm. The ball in my lower belly curled tighter, my legs and arms trembling, my cheeks soaked with tears.

The fingers on my clit moved faster, faster, faster, as did the two cocks inside me, and I shattered, screaming around Jack. Sparks exploded against my blackened vision, my body overloaded at the sensations.

"Damn, I love you." Jack ran a hand over my cheek, grinning from ear to ear as he wiped my tears away with his thumb.

Both of Eddy's hands were wrapped around my waist, holding me still as he pounded into me. "Do you know what happens when an alpha comes, Remi?"

I nodded faintly. I knew exactly what happened—had fantasized about it several times over the years.

"I'm going to knot you, and you are going to take it because you're a good fucking girl."

"That's right, baby," Jack said, his grip tightening on my face.

Two more thrusts and I felt it—Eddy's swelling inside me. I whimpered around Jack as Eddy grew and grew, stretching wide—*too* wide. It was too much, too good.

This is going to kill me.

He growled, his grip tightening around my waist to the point of bruises as he spilled inside of me. Jack followed right after, and I swallowed him down in a lust-induced delirium.

Good Ghouls, did I just die?

My arms and legs gave out, but they caught me, rolling me onto my side with Eddy still knotted inside me, his hand running up and down my spine. Jack threw his jacket over me before lying down in front of me and wiping my sweat-soaked hair from my face to kiss my forehead.

I smiled drunkenly and placed my hand on top of his, my eyes closing as I slipped further and further into sleep.

Acknowledgments

HUGE thank you to Damon Salvatore, Jack Skellington, the bikers on TikTok, Chase Atlantic, Halloweentown, and literally every masked man ever.

Oh, and KC Hayes—thank you for sending me all those inspiration videos and feeding into my ego every day without fail <3

About the Author

J.D. Linton is the Amazon Bestselling debut author of The Last Storm, book 1 in the Rogue x Ara series.

She's married to her high school sweetheart and a mother of one. She enjoys reading and writing spicy fantasy romance, and as with most writing mamas, she's also a midnight writer—up all day with her real baby and up all night with her fictional babies. When not writing, you can find her reading, making a million TikToks, or at the park with her son.

Writing has truly changed her life, and she's even more thankful for the incredible community it brought with it.